A Murder Most Unlikely

Mrs. Lillywhite Investigates

Book Five

Emily Queen

Willow Hill BOOKS

A Murder Most Unlikely

Copyright © 2020 by Emily Queen

ISBN- 978-1-953044-25-9

Contents

British Terms

Bank holiday - national holiday

Bin - trash can

Block of flats - apartment building

Bloody - an intensifying mild expletive (swear word)

Bollocks - dismay or disbelief

Boot (of a car) – trunk

Cheeky - endearingly rude or disrespectful

Chemist's - drugstore/pharmacy

Cupboard – closet

Cuppa - cup of (usually tea)

Daft - a bit stupid or silly

Diamante – rhinestone

Fancy - a verb expressing desire ("do you fancy some dinner?")

Flat - apartment

Footway – sidewalk

Garden - yard

Ground floor - first floor

High street - main street

Holiday - vacation

Lift - elevator

Lorry - truck

Petrol - gas (for a car)

Post - mail

Rubbish - garbage
Timetable - schedule
Wanker - a jerk
Worktop – countertop

~Find more British English terms on my website~

A Murder Most Unlikely

ONE

Rosemary Lillywhite stood, removed a handkerchief from her pocket, and wiped the sweat from her brow before resuming her efforts to dislodge a trunk from the recesses of the attic. London had been exceptionally balmy that year, and all the heat had risen to the townhouse's top floor to create a miserably sweltering experience. She could hear Wadsworth pacing from the level below, and when he called out to her for the fifth time since the beginning of her expedition, she could barely contain her irritation.

"I'm quite all right," Rosemary reassured the butler, poking her head out of the stairwell to prove she was still in one piece.

That his mistress insisted upon tending to the heavy lifting galled, but he knew from experience that once she got an idea into her head, she wouldn't budge no matter how reasonable the argument presented to her.

"It's my duty," Rosemary huffed. "I won't hear any more about it! Now go on, and leave me be." Her tone brooked no refusal.

With a sigh, Wadsworth meandered back down the corridor towards the stairs to the ground floor but refused to descend them until he was certain Rosemary truly needed no assistance. She knew the creak of every floorboard in the place and could tell he was still keeping a close watch, but she allowed him to stand guard without further argument.

"He means well," she muttered to herself, "but I'm perfectly capable of sorting through a few dusty old trunks."

Though Rosemary's tendency towards independence was one of her defining traits, in this case, it was less about stubbornness and more about a sense of obligation. After her husband Andrew passed away unexpectedly a little more than a year before, she hadn't the heart to attend to the distribution and disposal of his belongings.

To make room for an art studio, she'd moved the furniture around in the office where he'd worked as a private detective, but Rosemary had disposed of nothing even there. Now, it was time for a bigger change, and it simply wouldn't feel right for anyone else to complete the task.

When a commotion sounded from the ground floor, Wadsworth hesitated before descending the stairs to find Rosemary's brother, Frederick, and her best friend, Vera Blackburn, on the doorstep. The pair had recently become inseparable, much to Rosemary's delight and Vera's surprise. After welcoming them into the entrance hall, Wadsworth appealed to the one person he knew might persuade Rosemary to leave her post.

"Good afternoon, Mr. Woolridge," he said politely and turned to Vera. "Perhaps you could fetch the mistress from the attic. She's insisted upon sorting through Mr. Andrew's trunks, and—"

"And she won't let you lend a hand of assistance," Vera finished the sentence for him with a wry smile. "That sounds just like Rosemary. I'll see to it." With that, she marched up the stairs leaving Frederick behind.

"Rosie, dear, did you forget you invited us for tea?" Vera asked when she laid eyes on her friend. "Why don't you come down from there? You look a fright!"

"Thank you ever so much," Rosemary retorted, her voice muffled due to the fact that she'd resumed her thorough search of the trunk, and her head had nearly disappeared into its depths. When she pulled it back out again, her hair crackled with static electricity and stuck up in every direction.

Holding back a giggle, Vera helped her friend off the floor and gently guided her down the stairs. "This can wait, can't it? I'm starved, and your brother is probably already pilfering gin from your drinks cart. The fact that it's not yet noon doesn't appear to have occurred to him," Vera said, a note of amusement in her voice. "He's taking full advantage of the bank holiday weekend."

Rosemary's mouth tipped into an affectionate smile. "That sounds like Frederick," she said as she and Vera, arms linked, walked into the dining room where tea had already been laid out.

"What exactly sounds like me?" Frederick asked, raising a glass of clear liquid to his lips with a mischievous smile. The lock of golden ringlet that usually dangled into his face had been trimmed into submission, but he brushed at the spot anyway out of habit. Eyes the same blue as Rosemary's twinkled when his gaze landed on Vera, and the look that passed between the new couple made her sublimely happy and a tiny bit sad at the same time.

"Oh, we were just discussing your finer points, dear brother," Rosemary said affectionately. "Sobriety not being among them."

Frederick shrugged, drained the glass, and winked at his sister. "Sobriety is for the horses. Now, let's get down to the business of this weekend. I'm due back to work in a few days, and I'd like to return with some happy and, with any luck, scandalous memories. There must be a party brewing somewhere in London that would fit the bill."

"Oh!" Vera said, then spun on her heel and strode back to the entrance hall, returning a few moments later with her handbag. "I've got six tickets to an art opening. My understudy in the play, Daisy, has some pieces on display, and she said it's sure to be a swell affair. She's been through some hard times, and I'd like to support her. Do you think Max would enjoy something like that? Perhaps we could ask Abigail and Martin if they want the last two tickets."

Rosemary noted how Frederick's nose scrunched and how he made certain Vera didn't catch the slip. She doubted an art gallery opening was what he'd had in mind when he suggested a wild party, but he was bright enough to realize he'd better go along with whatever the women suggested.

"I had lunch with Abigail yesterday," Rosemary said, "and she's simply dying to get out of the house for an evening. I suspect she's quite lonely. Ever since the murder investigation was closed, Martin has seen a marked increase in business. It seems people are more intrigued than concerned over the *Killer Dentist of Park Road.*"

When Rosemary had solved the murder and cleared Martin's name, she hadn't expected to make friends in the process, but a good friend indeed Abigail had proved herself to be.

"And Max?" Vera pressed.

The thought of the handsome detective inspector Max Whittington brought a smile to Rosemary's face. After solving yet *another* murder, they had shared one perfect kiss, and she was still flying high from the experience.

"I don't think it will be difficult to persuade him, assuming he's free. He's been swamped with cases, and we haven't had a chance to see much of one another since we returned to London. This would be our first official date."

"Something tells me Max will make certain he's free for you, Rosie. He's besotted, don't you think, Freddie?" Vera demanded.

"Not as besotted as I am with you, darling," Frederick replied smoothly. Rosemary had to give him credit for understanding exactly what made a woman tick. Of course, he'd had plenty of practice before the realization that Vera was *the one*, and it helped that as Rosemary's oldest friend, the two had grown up together. Their sense of familiarity was equally comforting and disconcerting at this early stage of their romance.

Vera's mother had always had a soft spot for Frederick and thoroughly approved of him for her daughter. For once, however, Lorraine hadn't been a force of influence on Evelyn Woolridge. Convincing Rosemary and Frederick's mother to accept the match turned into a nightmare of biblical proportions. All was well now, though, and it seemed a ray of hope had chased away most of the darkness in which Rosemary had been mired since Andrew's death.

A date with Max might help blow away the last of the cobwebs.

Of course, she'd always remember the love she shared with Andrew, but life was too short to allow the loss to become crippling. He'd want her to move on—though whether he'd be thrilled that the object of her affection was his closest mate, she couldn't say and had decided to dispense with the question altogether.

"Well, speak of the devil," Frederick said when the doorbell chimed, and the detective inspector in question strode into the room. He shook Max's hand and clapped him on the back. "Good to see you, my friend."

Max returned the handshake and the greeting, all the while his eyes flicking to Rosemary's. "I see the whole gang's here," he quipped. "Should I be worried?"

Rosemary allowed him to take her hand in his for a fleeting moment, and her heart fluttered.

"All's well here, Inspector," Frederick replied, though Max's question hadn't been meant for him to answer. "Simply smashing, actually, though I fear we've been roped into a dreadfully boring evening of artistic pomp and circumstance."

At Max's questioning look, Rosemary explained. "We've got tickets to an art opening tomorrow night. Are you, by some chance, free?" she asked coyly.

"Yes, as a matter of fact," Max said, flushing. "That's why I'm here, though I didn't intend to invite you out on a date with your brother and Vera watching."

Frederick let out a guffaw. "You might as well get used to it."

"Yes, I suppose so," Max replied with a rueful grin. "As long as dinner is part of the plan. I'll make reservations and meet you lot here tomorrow evening." He bade them all goodbye and left the townhouse with a spring in his step.

"It's settled, then," Vera exclaimed when he was gone. "Now, we must shop!"

Shopping was Vera's solution for everything, though, in this instance, Rosemary was more than happy to oblige.

Two

More often than not, shopping with Vera ended up an excursion to rival that of a search for the holy grail, and this instance proved no exception. Several dresses, even more pairs of shoes, a couple of handbags, and enough stockings to outfit a dance troupe filled the boot of Rosemary's car to bursting. Wadsworth helped the pair out of the back seat and shooed them inside, insisting on carrying everything himself.

"I'm terribly sorry, Wadsworth." Vera winked at the butler, bringing a blush to his cheeks.

"It's quite all right, Miss Vera. In fact, I'd say it's a sign that the mistress has begun to shake her doldrums." He set about his work while Rosemary shook her head at her friend.

"He's got a soft spot for you," she said, amused.

Vera waved a hand. "He's a dear, and he takes care of you." She smiled at Anna, Rosemary's maid, who had come to assist Wadsworth with the packages. "We have a certain unspoken understanding about that. That he could shoot a flea off a dog's back from fifty paces makes me feel better about you being virtually alone in this big house."

"I told you, you're welcome to move in whenever you'd like," Rosemary said lightly. It was a conversation they'd had many times before. Though Vera's insistence Rosemary would tire of her constant presence and annoying quirks might have been valid, she suspected that now, the reluctance had more to do with the budding relationship between Vera and Frederick than anything else.

"Once I've cleaned out Andrew's things, there will be much more room."

When Vera's face contorted into a pained expression, Rosemary wondered if perhaps she'd been wrong after all. Perhaps Vera simply didn't relish the idea of sleeping in her friend's dead husband's rooms. Rosemary supposed she couldn't blame her for that and decided, at least for now, to let the subject drop.

"You know," Rosemary murmured to Vera on the way up the front steps, "I think I'm going to wear the dress I bought in Pardington after all. The peacock-colored one. What do you think?"

"I think it's perfect. You look like a cross between an angel and a devil in that dress, which I think will do quite nicely for your first real outing with Max. However, I don't regret the shopping trip for one moment. That turquoise turban I bought was worth the afternoon of scouring alone. Anna, could you please hang everything in Rosie's room? You're simply going to die when you see the dresses we bought, and there's a little something in there for you as well."

Anna's round face lit with pleasure. "Thank you, Miss Vera. You certainly didn't have to think of me."

"Well, I did, dear girl," Vera replied with a grin.

"You've taken a shine to her as well as Wadsworth, I see," Rosemary commented after Anna was out of earshot.

Vera shrugged. "She's a good girl, and it won't be long

before some nice young man realizes it, sweeps her off her feet and leaves you in search of a new maid."

"I suppose you're right," Rosemary said with a furrowed brow. "I believe I'll leave that as a problem for another day."

Hours later, Rosemary descended the stairs to the ground floor of the townhouse amid whistles and catcalls from Frederick and Vera. She'd allowed Anna to help sweep her hair into a complicated yet understated up-do, with golden tendrils cascading around her face. The dress, a thigh-length number in cerulean and violet, set off the blue of her eyes, which had been carefully outlined in black kohl.

"You look positively ravishing!" Vera exclaimed as Rosemary grinned and spun in a circle.

Frederick grunted and drew himself up to his full height. "You do look lovely, Rosie dear, but now I'm having second thoughts about passing you off to the inspector. It is a brother's duty, you know, to protect his sister at all costs."

"I think you can let your guard down, Freddie. Max is hardly a Lothario."

"I'm not certain whether to take that as a compliment or an insult," came Max's voice from behind Rosemary. He must have slipped inside when she wasn't looking, and she whirled around to face him standing in her doorway for the second time in as many days. When his mouth hung open for a moment longer than expected, she raised an eyebrow.

Max stuttered, "You look—you look wonderful, Rosemary."

The statement brought a blush to her cheeks, making her appear all the prettier. "Shall we?" she asked, pushing the awkward moment aside.

"Yes, let's. I managed to call in a favor and got us reservations for eight o'clock at Kettner's," Max said. Vera let out a sigh of appreciation. One of the more popular establishments in London, Kettner's tended to be solidly booked for weeks ahead.

"Freddie, be a dear and fetch Abigail and Martin from next door," Rosemary implored. Frederick nodded and clasped Vera's hand. The two of them exited to the street, allowing Max and Rosemary a moment alone.

"You really are lovely," Max said when they were gone, brushing a lock of hair away from her face. He stared into her eyes with an expression of wonder, but it seemed Abigail had been waiting at the door. When her lilting voice drifted inside far too soon, the spell was broken, and Rosemary reluctantly followed Max out.

Abigail had gone all out with her appearance, wearing a drop-waisted sage green frock that, although not as flashy as Rosemary's, complemented her ginger hair and hazel eyes. Martin kept a protective hand on the small of her back, looking quite dashing in a suit and tie.

"Rosemary, that dress is simply marvelous!" Abigail said as she took it in, eliciting another round of compliments.

"We do look a fashionable group, don't we?" Vera commented happily. "Now, let's get going. I'm starved!"

"We'll be right behind you lot," Abigail promised as Martin, always a gentleman, closed the car door behind her. However, when the foursome arrived at the restaurant, the Redberrys' car did not immediately appear.

Inside, the maitre d' sniffed when Max explained that only four of the six guests had arrived.

"Apologies, sir, but we cannot seat you until your entire

party is present. You're welcome to wait in the champagne bar. However, we cannot hold the table for long."

"Wherever could they have gone?" Vera asked, looking around for the sage-colored dress Abigail had been wearing.

Rosemary shrugged and glanced sideways. "Perhaps they've made a wrong turn or had a breakdown. They wouldn't want us to let it ruin the evening, and I'm certain they'll be along eventually."

Having followed her gaze, Vera said with a grin, "You aren't fooling me, Rosie. I know for a fact you can't resist a trip to the champagne bar."

"One can understand why she might feel that way," Max interjected as they entered the space. A circular bar dominated the room, cushioned stools offering a reprieve from the tight pinch of a heeled shoe, and crystal chandeliers lit everything with a romantic glow.

Within moments, the barman placed a glass of champagne in front of each of them, and Frederick raised his in a toast. "To old friends and new beginnings."

"Hear, hear!" the rest chorused in unison. Rosemary felt a prick behind her eyes and blinked back tears so as not to smudge her makeup. Across the room, the sight of Abigail and Martin's arrival interrupted the moment.

"We didn't lose our table, did we?" Martin huffed. "Somehow, we got caught behind a broken-down lorry and were rerouted halfway across town!"

Max glanced towards the door where the maitre d' beckoned. "It looks like you made it in the nick of time."

On her way to the dining room, Rosemary plucked a matchbook scrawled with the name Kettner's from a plate on top of the bar and tucked it into her handbag as a memento from the evening.

"I simply must powder my nose," Vera announced once the table had been secured. "Rosemary, Abigail, won't you accompany me?" The restroom was nearly as opulent as the champagne bar, with satin wallpaper and gilt-framed mirrors.

"Tell me, Rosemary, how is your evening with Max going?" Abigail asked when they were alone. "I almost feel as though we're all intruding on your rendezvous."

Rosemary brushed aside her concerns. "It's lovely, and to be quite honest, I'm as nervous as a teenager. Having you all here makes it easier. I can't remember the last time I was this happy. There are no pending murder investigations and no dead bodies lying around. It's a welcome change."

Checking her appearance one last time, Vera patted a stray hair into place. "I suppose we'd better get back out there before Freddie decides to order for us. He has the most appalling taste in cuisine."

At the table, Rosemary chose the pâté appetizer, followed by the coq au vin, and sat back to enjoy the pleasant, lively conversation.

"What exactly is this exhibit we're attending?" Martin asked. "Abigail doesn't know a Picasso painting from a Michaelangelo sculpture, so her relay of the details was rather unhelpful." He tossed her an adoring look to let her know he was only poking fun.

"It's a new gallery owned by a man named Sidney Mariott," Vera explained. "The exhibit will feature two new artists, one of whom is a friend of mine. But the real coup de grâce is a recovered Renoir—a portrait of a young girl—that will be on display.

It's one of the artist's missing works, and it's supposed to be spectacular. I don't know how this Mr. Mariott got hold of it, but from what I hear, he paid a pretty penny."

When Frederick barely concealed a snort, Rosemary burned him with a look and said to Vera, "That sounds exciting."

Vera swallowed a bite of her chicken, gave Frederick a side-eyed look, and said, "According to Daisy, there have been rumblings about a protest. Apparently, the other artist's work is quite sensual, and there's a contingency of people who believe the exhibit is too lewd for public display. I suppose we'll see for ourselves soon enough."

"Lewd paintings? Why didn't you say so before? That puts the whole caper in a different light." Frederick earned himself another glare.

Abigail's eyes lit up, and she grinned widely. "I, for one, agree with Frederick! It sounds positively thrilling." A chorus of agreement went round the table.

"Max, how is your mother doing?" Rosemary asked Max, changing the subject. She explained to the rest of the group that Ariadne Whittington had recently moved to London from the country where she and Max's late father had kept a large home with even more expansive gardens.

"The woman has gone completely batty!" he exclaimed. "She's convinced herself that her new neighbor is a deranged psychopath and that he's plotting murder against his wife! I've no idea what's given her cause to believe such a thing, but I'm beginning to worry for her sanity."

"Perhaps London isn't agreeing with her," Rosemary postulated.

Max grimaced. "What she needs is to find a new hobby, but

with her hip injury, I don't know what. She certainly can't play croquet anymore, and I know how that must gall. She was quite good once upon a time."

"It must be difficult giving up her old life, and she's used to having a lot more work to occupy her time."

"That's the crux of the problem, Rose," Max agreed. "You hit the nail on the head. She's never been bored a day in her life, and now she's too much time on her hands."

Looking forward to viewing scandalous artwork, Frederick chivvied the rest along until Vera found it necessary to jam the heel of her pump into his instep.

"Ow!" he exclaimed but took the hint and let the rest of the meal pass in polite conversation.

THREE

When Rosemary stepped out of the car near the corner upon which the Mariott gallery stood, it was to find herself in a part of London she hadn't frequented since her art school days, and a wave of nostalgia rolled over her. She could almost, out of the corner of her eye, picture younger versions of herself and Vera tripping over the cobbled streets that made walking in heels a treacherous prospect. The lampposts stationed at every block told a story of the last few years if one were to peel away the inch-thick layer of leaflets tacked to them one strip at a time.

Off to the side of the building, scores of people milled about in the footway, two distinct groups discerning themselves even as Rosemary looked on. Most were obviously anxious to get inside for a peek at the deceased famous artist's newly recovered painting. A smaller contingency huddled around a man of average build and even more average appearance, whose intent was, evidently, to get his cronies all riled up.

"Those must be the protesters," Rosemary commented to Max as he led her and her friends towards the entrance.

The ringleader confirmed her musing when he shouted, "Take down the abomination!"

A chorus of chanting requests to remove the obscenity

prompted innocent bystanders to back away with expressions running the gamut from fright to irritation.

Just when the frenzy reached its peak, the gallery doors burst open and out through them came a formidable-looking man with arms the size of tree trunks. His gait suggested anger, though his face remained impassive—almost bored, as if fending off an irate mob was an everyday occurrence.

"Sod off, Chas! And take your cronies with 'ya!" he drawled and glared.

The man called Chas raised his fist in the air, puffed out his chest, and hollered back, "You sod off, you wanker, we'll do as we like. We're not breaking any laws, and you know it."

Max wrapped a protective arm around Rosemary, sidestepping the argument, and then ushered the group through the entrance. Inside, the space was barren save for the pieces on display. Whitewashed walls ensured nothing diverted attention away from the art, though from her cursory glance, it became clear that this was not the type of work that normally appealed to Rosemary.

Her tastes ran towards contemporary lines and abstract shapes, though she appreciated the way Renoir's impressionist works teased the senses. She smiled wryly to herself and tucked an idea into the back of her mind. Later, when she was alone, she would explore that thought and apply it toward creating her own masterpiece.

Turning her attention back to her friends, Rosemary's smile widened at Max's expression. She peeked at the piece that had caught his eye—a nude portrait of a woman that she had to admit landed somewhat to the left of tasteful.

At a quick glance, the woman's form seemed to drape

elegantly across a garden bench flanked by roses. Upon closer inspection, Rosemary's discerning eye picked out elements of several painting styles. The light and shading on the main figure could have been lifted from a Renaissance master. What pushed the spread-legged figure closer toward lewd than artful were the hands placed below and lifting the breasts, the slitted eyes looking directly at the viewer without a shred of modesty.

The arbor and roses were done in a graphic, art nouveau style, each flower a splash of red, but the petals outlined in black lacked any of the same sense of light and shadow as the figure they framed. The two styles jarred the senses, but not in the way Rosemary felt good art should do.

Max watched Rosemary study the painting, his eyes flicking from her to it, and then back again.

Finally, having decided she'd seen enough, she turned to him. "Are you all right?" she asked, barely able to control the giggle threatening to escape her lips.

"Of course," Max said, shaking his head and turning away from the spectacle. "Though I believe I might need a drink." To that, Martin vehemently agreed, though Frederick seemed quite content with the view. He only went reluctantly when the other two men left on a mission to find gin, leaving Rosemary, Vera, and Abigail to peruse the art.

"You'd think we'd dragged them into a den of iniquity." Vera commented with a grin. "Or worse, took them knicker shopping."

"I didn't realize I was married to such a fuddy duddy," Abigail agreed.

"At least the two of you aren't here on a first date," Rosemary said, unable to control her laughter.

Vera poked her in the ribs between fits. "You'll have quite the story to tell the grandchildren if this all works out."

The trio made a concerted effort to suppress their giggles and returned their attention to the art.

"I thought your friend Daisy had pieces in this gallery?" Rosemary asked Vera after peering at several of the labels. "Most of these are done by someone named Reno Riley."

Vera's brow furrowed. "Yes, I see that. Perhaps her pieces are on the other side and we simply haven't made it all the way around. Oh, look, the men are back with drinks." Indeed, Max, Frederick, and Martin wove their way through the crowd, finally depositing gin and tonics into the ladies' hands.

Max's arm went around Rosemary's waist as the group continued to meander through the gallery, each of them becoming less impressed the farther into the throng they wove.

"Am I simply daft, or is this Reno Riley's work as terrible as I think it is?" Frederick asked Vera under his breath loud enough for Rosemary to hear.

"It's not you, brother dear," she said. "This time, anyway. Ignoring the content for a moment, the quality of the brush strokes is untrained at best. Still, if he aimed to elicit shock as the primary response to the work, then he's succeeded." The critique was as balanced as Rosemary could make it.

"Oh, thank goodness," Abigail spoke up. "I thought perhaps I was the only one!"

"Why don't we make our way back around to the exit as quickly as possible," Frederick implored and received a chorus of agreement.

When Max's arm tightened suddenly around Rosemary's waist, she turned to face him only to find his gaze fixed on something across the room. His eyes widened and then he shot an apologetic glance at her before the woman—for the something was a woman—parted the crowd to approach him. Her skin was deeply tanned, as if she'd just come back from holiday, and there was something exotic about her green, almond-shaped eyes and thick black lashes.

"Max Whittington. It has been far too long!" the woman said, quite breathlessly indeed, once she arrived. Rosemary couldn't tell if she was winded or simply putting it on, but the way Vera's eyes narrowed answered the question handily.

"Aurora, good to see you," Max replied stiffly, his nose crinkling at the assault of perfume that wafted around the woman. "This is Rosemary Lillywhite, my date." He said the last bit pointedly, and made no attempt to introduce the rest of his companions who were, by now, watching with the avid curiosity of unapologetic snoops.

"Yes, yes, lovely to meet you," Aurora said vaguely, only gracing Rosemary with a cursory glance. Had it not been for the obvious discomfiture of Max, Rosemary might have been bothered by the display. As it was, she found it mildly irritating to have their imminent escape interrupted. Her love for art in all forms aside, she would far rather have been seated at a dimly lit pub, enjoying the atmosphere amongst good friends. The champagne bar at Kettner's flashed through her thoughts, and suddenly she wished they'd stayed there instead.

"Let me introduce you to the owner of the gallery. He's also my fiancé." Aurora winked, grabbed Max's hand, and pulled him away from the rest of the group, leaving Rosemary no choice but to follow.

Four

"Sidney, darling," Aurora raised her voice when she found him in the crowd, a willowy, fair-skinned man with hair oiled into a slick style.

When he turned to face her, his expression held pleasure and a tinge of annoyance, but he wrapped up the conversation he'd been having and greeted her with an indulgent smile. "Hullo, hullo," Sidney said, holding out a hand to meet Max's outstretched one.

"This is Max Whittington and his friend, Rosemary. Max is an old beau of mine, a detective inspector for Scotland Yard! Isn't that exciting?"

Sidney's eyes widened and Rosemary thought he looked a little paler than he had before, if that was possible. She paid the fact little mind, her attention having been caught by what Aurora had let slip—she used to date Max, which accounted for the way he'd stiffened at the sight of her. More than ever, she wished they'd decided on a more intimate first rendezvous, but since there was nothing to be done about it now, she greeted Sidney politely and avoided eye contact with both Aurora and Max.

"This is your gallery?" she asked, glancing around. "It's a lovely space, and though we haven't made it around to see it up close yet, the Renoir looks spectacular." With a crowd constantly shifting in front of the coveted painting, Rosemary had managed only glimpses at the canvas. The only thing to do, she decided, would be to return at a later date when she could spend a quiet hour taking in every nuance.

Sidney's eyes flashed and flicked to the painting. "Yes, well, how could it not? I'd hoped it would draw in a crowd and boost the reputations of the other artists in one fell swoop, but so far, it's the only piece anyone cares about," he said, tossing a glance at one of the nudes painted by Reno Riley. "Perhaps the collection could have been more cohesive."

"Mr. Riley does seem to have a one-track mind," Rosemary mused. "Renoir produced a variety of works that were intended to celebrate all types of beauty. He didn't focus solely on that of the female form." She blushed, and added, "As I'm certain you already know."

"Ah, I suspect you've some artistic ability yourself. Am I right?" Sidney asked, becoming animated once again.

"I dabble," Rosemary replied modestly.

Sidney cocked his head to one side. "And a humble artist at that. Aren't many of those amongst us *dabblers*."

Aurora swatted him playfully on the arm. "You're more than a dabbler. It's *your* work you should be displaying."

With a laugh, Sidney brushed her off. "I keep telling her it's terribly bad form to open a gallery that showcases one's own work. Besides, I'm mediocre at best. Just can't seem to stay away from the scene. I do hope this opening goes well, however, or I'll be out on the streets peddling caricatures for a farthing apiece."

"Oh, you're far too modest yourself, darling. See, here's Sadie, she'll attest the fact."

Sadie Dawson turned out to be Sidney's receptionist, a nervous woman with a habit of wringing her hands together and, judging by the state of her nails, picking at her cuticles.

"Sidney," she said tersely, "there's a problem and I need you." She nodded towards the back of the room and Sidney sighed.

"My work is never finished. Lovely to have met you both. Perhaps we'll have time for a drink later." His tone apologetic, he tottered along after Sadie, towering over her while she explained whatever problem she needed solving. Sadie nodded a few times and then ascended the set of stairs leading to whatever rooms occupied the upper floor.

"I suppose I ought to go see if there's anything I can do to help her," Aurora said apologetically, though the sentiment fell on Rosemary with some relief.

When she and Max were alone, Rosemary raised an eyebrow. "An old beau?"

"I'm sorry, Rose. I'll explain all about Aurora later," Max promised. "I had no idea she would be here, I hope you know that."

"I do," Rosemary assured him. "It isn't as though you were the one to suggest this opening. Perhaps, in the future, we'll protest more strenuously when Vera arranges an outing. For now, let's not allow it to ruin our night. Freddie is probably halfway pickled already. We'd better go check on him." She led him to where Vera's bright turquoise turban bobbed above the throng.

"There you are," Vera exclaimed. "I want you to meet my

friend Daisy Kent. This is one of her pieces." She indicated a lovely painting done in the impressionist style, of a woman seated at a dressing table, her image reflected in the mirror.

Rosemary stepped back to take it in and then looked at Daisy appraisingly. "This is beautiful work. It evokes a sense of vulnerability and self-doubt, as though she's unsure of her beauty."

"Thank you so much," Daisy said, brightening infinitesimally. "That's exactly what I was attempting to convey. Although, with only three of my pieces making it into the opening, I doubt anyone will notice."

Vera's eyes darkened. "It's a travesty. Whoever owns this place needs to take a lesson in art history."

"It's that man over there." Rosemary pointed to where Sidney stood in a corner flanked by Aurora and another man. "The tall, gangly one who looks like he just swallowed a frog."

"That's him, all right, and the one yelling at him is Reno, the other artist," Daisy explained. "Though, what he has to be upset about, I couldn't fathom."

Frederick let out a half laugh, half grunt. "He's probably overheard some of the reactions to his work. The comments haven't been overly full of praise, but Daisy's contributions earned high marks all around."

Less deep in his cups than Rosemary expected, Frederick patted Daisy awkwardly on the shoulder and tilted his head to the side to peruse the nearest painting again.

"This Reno fellow seems to be obsessed with the female form, and on that I can't fault him, even though the finished product strikes me as somewhat unsavory. Your work is far more tasteful, but not at all boring. If this opening had been dedicated to you, I wouldn't have spent the last hour searching for the exit."

Daisy smiled, and her face lit up. It changed her entire appearance, and now Rosemary could see why she'd been picked as the understudy to Vera's role. The young woman's medium-toned hair and even features, seemingly nondescript at first, were very much like a blank canvas. A little color across her cheeks, some artful shading around the eyes and mouth, and it was a face that would transform into great beauty or the lack of same with equal ease.

"You have a fine hand with building impasto, Daisy." When Max gave Rosemary a questioning look, she took the explanation deeper. "Layers of paint built up to create the suggestion of line and shadow. See how Daisy has built stroke after brush stroke in subtle shades of color to create a sense of diffused light coming in from the left? Very fine work, and restful to view."

"Ahh, a woman who knows her art." The statement was made by a stout, moustachioed man in a tweed suit who appeared to pop up out of nowhere.

"Hello, Mr. Banks," Daisy said politely. "Seeing anything you like?"

"Actually, I have. Your pieces are simply smashing. I can't understand why you're not the headliner for this show. Your work deserves to be displayed prominently, and I can help with that if you'll let me."

His eyes twinkled, and he tossed a wink in Daisy's direction while waving around a pair of pince-nez that never seemed to make it onto the bridge of his nose.

She took the overture in stride, brushing it off, and said, "I'll think about your offer, Mr. Banks."

"You do that, Miss Kent. You have my card."

"What was that all about?" Vera asked Daisy once Mr. Banks had tottered off.

She waved a hand. "That was Arthur Banks. He's a gallery owner with a smaller space across town. I get the feeling I'm not the only artist he's trying to pilfer. Perhaps I ought to have listened to him after all, but I don't care for his methods. Creeping around other galleries looking for talent—it feels dishonest. Though I suppose it might be preferable to having my work diminished in favor of someone like Reno Riley." She sighed. "Especially now, with my mother in ill health. She needs a full-time nurse, and I was counting on the proceeds from this show to lighten the burden."

"Do consider the offer, Daisy dear," Vera implored. "That man might not have the draw of a Renoir painting at his gallery, but at least he has sense enough to realize you're the one with the talent in this room. Perhaps he'll write up a more lucrative offer."

Daisy's eyebrows furrowed as she considered what Vera had said, but then she spotted Reno Riley heading in their direction and said quickly, "I'll think about it, but for now I must go mingle. Why don't we plan on going for a drink after rehearsal this week? Perhaps Rod will accompany us."

With a suggestive eyebrow wiggle, she walked away to loiter near her pieces. Before long, Rosemary saw her speaking animatedly to a woman who appeared to admire her work.

As Rosemary and her friends drifted towards the door, Frederick turned to Vera and raised a quizzical brow. "Rod?"

"You know good and well that Rod Stone is my co-star in the play. He said he might attend the opening as a show of support for Daisy, but I haven't seen him yet nor do I care to. I vote that we dispense with the chitchat and get out of here before Reno shows up to ask our opinion of his work," Vera suggested. "I don't think I could be charitable in my estimation."

Upon that point, the six friends agreed.

FIVE

Escape proved more difficult than expected when Vera's worst fear came true. Catching her arm before she'd managed to cover half the distance to the door, Reno Riley gave Vera an appraising look that left her feeling coated with something slimy. "And who might you be?" he asked in what he probably thought was a suave manner.

"My date," Frederick quickly answered for her, his tone acerbic and bordering on hostile. "And you'd be wise to unhand her unless you'd like to be thrown to the wolves outside." He nodded towards the entrance, where the group of protesters had tightened around the building.

Reno removed his hands from Vera and held them up in surrender. "Relax, chap. I meant no harm. Simply getting to know my fans, that's all."

"We're here to see Daisy's pieces," Vera spat. "Yours would be better suited adorning the walls of a brothel."

"Whoa!" Reno replied. "You've got yourself a bearcat there, don't you?" he said to Frederick with a smarmy wink.

Frederick laughed, and the tension melted. "Yeah, I do, and she'll eat you alive, mate."

The artist backed off after taking one last, long look at Vera, and sauntered away.

"Oh, look, there's Rod now," Vera said, watching as Reno

stopped short on his way towards the actor, who stood next to Daisy near one of her paintings. Sidney and Reno both converged upon Rod at the same time, and a short conversation ensued. Frederick was too busy appraising the famously handsome Rod Stone to notice anything else, but Rosemary watched the entire exchange with interest.

First, Daisy gestured between Rod and Sidney as though she were introducing the two men, and then left them to speak with someone who looked like a potential buyer. A jovial smile plastered on his face, Sidney greeted Rod with a hearty handshake while Reno only offered a slight bob of the head.

Once the introductions seemed to be over, the three men moved to stand in front of Reno's paintings, and a new discussion began. One that didn't appear to be to Sidney's liking. His complexion growing ruddier by the moment, Sidney's glance swiveled between Reno and Rod. After a few moments, he grabbed Reno by the arm and practically dragged him away into a far corner where a short but heated conversation ensued.

Rosemary wondered if, after tonight, the question of whether Daisy had to share billing with Reno would be moot. The two men looked as though they might resort to fisticuffs if the tension rose another notch.

When the exchange was over, Reno turned and sauntered away. Sidney glared daggers at his back, but Reno, who now faced Rosemary's group, appeared quite pleased with himself.

Rival gallery owner Arthur Banks chose the wrong moment to approach Sidney, who spat something at him and then turned on his heel and stalked towards the center of the room and the Renoir. He took a long look at it and then spoke a few words to one of the onlookers before noticing the backlog at the entrance. Sidney's face twisted again into an irritated expression, and he shoved through the crowd without much consideration for his guests.

Having seen enough for one evening, Rosemary linked arms with Max on one side and Frederick on the other. Whether the protest had backfired and brought art lovers out in droves or Sydney had done an admirable job of filling the gallery for the opening, she couldn't say, but the place was packed tighter than a nightclub serving free gin.

"Come along, now."

Plowing through the crowd seemed the only option, and she'd gladly mow the rest of the guests over if it meant getting to the door any faster. With so many people in the room, the air had begun to feel close and too warm for comfort.

Freedom, however, was not meant to be. As Rosemary and her friends came in sight of the door, they discovered the hulking man who'd been guarding the entrance now standing inside. Next to him, Aurora wrung her hands in distress. Looking more annoyed than ever, Sidney snapped out a comment that made Sadie's face turn pale.

"Max!" Aurora's shout beckoned him over. "You're just the person we need right now. Please say you can help. What started out as a peaceful protest has turned into a siege!"

Max turned to Rosemary. "Stay here, I'll see what I can do," he said and marching authoritatively to the door and pulled it open. Undaunted, or maybe merely too curious to wait, Rosemary and the rest of the group followed him.

Chas, the protester ringleader, pressed inside immediately, threatening to bring the rest of his wave of cronies with him.

Max firmly shut the door again, but not before Chas zeroed in on Sidney.

"What do you think of this, boss man? The people have a right to be heard! Your disregard for old-fashioned morals and values is despicable! How can you support an artistic movement that's lewd and inappropriate? Don't you care about the future of our children?"

Sidney's beady eyes widened in surprise, then narrowed. "Art is about pushing boundaries. It's about education and widening one's perspective. It's *supposed* to make people question the status quo!" Even during his staunch defense, the fear showed plainly on his face, and he backed away from Chas.

Aurora mimicked his movements, sticking close to her fiancé, leaving Sadie standing there looking horrified.

When Chas caught sight of her, his anger immediately seemed to dissipate. He stared dumbfounded at the woman as though she were some sort of angel descended from heaven. His mouth opened and closed, but no words escaped, and suddenly the fearful mood deflated.

"It's time for you to go," Max said sharply, "and take your friends with you."

Chas simply nodded, not taking his eyes off Sadie. The woman's face erupted into a blush, and her gaze fixed on the floor in avoidance.

"I'm sorry!" Chas directed his comment towards Sadie but took himself off without another outburst. Through the open door, he could be heard ordering the protesters away. The next ten minutes saw the street cleared and the congestion in the gallery dispersed enough for Rosemary and her friends to make good on their escape.

Six

Max mixed two drinks and then settled onto the sofa next to Rosemary, handing one to her. She stared at him for a few moments, unwilling to be the one to begin the conversation.

"I suppose you're wondering about my history with Aurora," he said, a note of hesitation in his voice.

"I suppose I am," she replied, "though it seems somewhat premature to have that discussion at this juncture. We haven't even finished our first official date. It isn't as though we're betrothed. You don't owe me an explanation, as long as she's in the past."

"Aurora is most definitely in the past," Max said decisively. "So far in the past, in fact, that I haven't thought about her in years. Still, I'd like to explain. We may not have made it through our date yet, but it's not as though we're strangers, either."

Rosemary laughed. "That is true. You've saved my life on more than one occasion. I'd say that puts us firmly out of the acquaintances category."

Max shifted in the seat, leaning forward to rest his elbows on his knees. "I dated Aurora for a few months several years ago, just after you and Andrew met. It was an ill-fated match from the beginning. She and I are complete opposites in every way. At first, it was exciting, but once the shine wore off, I knew we weren't meant to be together. Unfortunately, Aurora did not feel the same way."

He sounded embarrassed. "When I broke things off, she didn't take it well. I think she was expecting a proposal."

"Perhaps Frederick was right when he insinuated you're somewhat of a Lothario," Rosemary replied with a smile.

Max laughed, his eyes crinkling around the edges in a way that made Rosemary's heart flutter. "Hardly. I believe Aurora would have married anyone willing, and I rather would have preferred feeling like a first choice."

"You are a catch, Max Whittington, and contrary to your perception regarding Aurora's feelings, it seems I'm not the only one who's noticed."

"You're the only one I *want* to notice, Rose," he said, his voice turning low and husky. For a moment, it was as if the world stopped turning. Rosemary's breath quickened as Max leaned in and covered her lips with his own. The shock of his touch sent shivers up and down her spine, and she allowed herself to revel in the feeling. Too quickly, it was over, and Max appeared as shaken as she was.

"I do wonder if perhaps I wasn't entirely wrong in my youthful ideas about love," he said once his heart stopped racing. "When can I see you again?"

Rosemary raised an eyebrow and said coquettishly, "When would you *like* to see me again?"

A smile and a blush spreading across his face, Max replied, "How about tomorrow? My mother invited me to her cottage for brunch. Would you like to come along? She's been asking about you, and perhaps you could talk her out of this obsession with her neighbors since she won't listen to a word I say."

Part of her wanted to come up with a reasonable excuse to wiggle out of the invitation, but her desire to spend more time with him had Rosemary agreeing against her better judgment.

Once he'd gone, she went upstairs to get ready for bed. Moving quietly so as not to disturb young Anna in the room next door, she fished the matchbook from the restaurant out of her purse and propped it against a decorative bowl sitting on her nightstand where she could smile to herself every time she looked at it.

SEVEN

Rosemary nearly tore her hair out attempting to dress for Max's mother and was thankful she'd made better decisions than had Vera and Frederick the previous evening. The two of them would probably still be lounging in their beds by the time she returned to the townhouse after brunch. The quiet did nothing to calm her nerves, however, and by the time she'd chosen a mid-calf-length summer dress in cheery yellow, her dressing room looked as though a storm had blown through it.

After the third time she had to pull something back out that Anna had put away during the process, Rosemary banished the girl to the lower floors.

"But I should—" Anna protested.

"Thank you, I'll manage." Rosemary gently closed the door in Anna's face, smiling to herself when she heard a mumble of protest and then the sound of retreating feet. Some people— such as her mother—might say her staff took far too many liberties, but Anna had spunk. A trait of which Rosemary approved. Most of the time, anyway.

More than anything, Rosemary wanted to impress Ariadne Whittington. She had helped Max restore the flat where his mother would live out the rest of her days, making decorating suggestions she hoped would bring some joy to Mrs. Whittington's life.

Unfortunately, the woman hadn't exactly taken to Rosemary during their first meeting. On that occasion, she'd run into Max and his mother on their way into the theater, and Mrs. Whittington had made it quite clear that Rosemary's wallpaper choices weren't her cup of tea. Furthermore, she'd rushed Max off before even having the chance at a longer conversation, and the whole experience left Rosemary's stomach tied up in knots. She knew how important it was to Max to have harmony within a family, and even more so how highly he regarded his mother's opinion.

The looming worry that Ariadne would neither like nor accept her hung over Rosemary's head like a rumbling storm cloud.

"Best to get it over with now, I suppose," she said to herself. "Only time will tell."

Max rang the doorbell upon his arrival, like a gentleman, and offered her his arm as they descended the front doorstep.

"Thank you for agreeing to attend brunch with me. Mother has been pressing me for more details about you, and this way she can see for herself why I've become so enamored."

Rosemary blushed scarlet, unsure how to respond. Her first instinct was to ignore the comment, but Max deserved better than that and so she threw caution to the wind.

"She'll never believe I'm good enough for you. That's the way of mothers, though I do hope I'm wrong, for I'm quite smitten myself."

It was as bold a statement as she'd made to Max at this juncture in their relationship, and though she felt secure in his affections, she found it difficult to get the words out. Deciding nothing could be more heartbreaking than the pain she'd already been forced to endure, she smiled lightly and felt a little shiver of satisfaction at his dumbfounded expression.

"She'll adore you. How could she not?"

The exchange calmed Rosemary and she felt the concern of the morning drain away, leaving behind only hopeful anticipation.

Upon arriving at Mrs. Whittington's flat, Rosemary let out an exclamation of surprise. It was a modest little cottage house, not so unlike the two others it was situated between, save for the blooms cascading out of every available container and the vines twisting around the support columns.

"Oh my! It's been completely transformed! Did your mother do all this?" she asked incredulously.

Nodding, Max grinned and said, "Wait until you see the rear garden. It was the mad dash to get all the plants in that caused Mother to hurt her hip in the first place. Now, she's anxious to get back out there and finish her plans."

"It looks positively perfect to me," Rosemary replied, still ogling the climbing roses, and followed Max onto the veranda. When he opened the front door, out charged a little bulldog with a scrunched nose and soulful eyes. He bounced around near their feet until Max bent down to give him a pat on the head, and then the furry bundle took a turn with Rosemary.

She laughed and bent down to scratch behind his ears. The little dog put his head in her hand and stared up at her lovingly. "Not much of a guard dog, is he?"

"No, certainly not, are you, Duke?" Max replied with a wry smile and one last pat on the dog's head.

They found Ariadne Whittington in the sitting room, perched on what looked to Rosemary like an uncomfortable wooden chair. Laid out on the table in front of her was a tea tray, a pair of reading glasses, two books, a notebook and pencil, and a tube of hand salve. She didn't attempt to use the cane situated to her right and instead heaved herself up using the arms of the chair.

"Sit down, Mother, we'll come to you," Max said, but she brushed him off.

"Mind your manners, darling boy. I'll do what I want, and I'll hear nothing more about it." There was a sting to the words, but Rosemary could tell it had nothing to do with Max and everything to do with his mother's pride. Duke ran around Ariadne's chair a few times before settling down and cuddling up next to the spot where her feet had been.

"It's lovely to see you again, Mrs. Whittington." Rosemary stepped forward. "Thank you for the brunch invitation. I do hope it wasn't too much trouble."

Gruffly, Mrs. Whittington waved away Rosemary's comment. "Not too much. Been making brunch every Sunday for fifty years. I'm not nearly as lame as my son would have you believe. Quite capable, in fact, and my mind is sharp as a tack. Now, stand back and let me have a look at you." She appraised Rosemary from head to toe, then turned abruptly and headed for the kitchen.

Rosemary sent a panicked, questioning glance at Max. Her eyes narrowed when she noticed him trying to hide a smile.

"Don't worry, Rose," he whispered as he ushered her down the corridor behind his mother. "You passed her test. Trust me, you'd know if you hadn't. She's much more liable to hand out criticism than praise."

"Would you like any help, Mrs. Whittington?" Rosemary asked politely as they entered the kitchen.

"Just call me Ariadne, dear," she replied, pulling a layered cake out of the bread box on the worktop. "Even after all these years, being called Mrs. Whittington still makes me think my husband's mother is looking over my shoulder. Not that I'd be surprised if the woman had decided to haunt me for all eternity, mind you, but I find the thought somewhat disconcerting."

"Ariadne." The request seemed like a step in the right direction, but Ariadne's next comment cast some doubt upon the proceedings.

"You can carry that tray into the dining room if you like. I know it's not as fancy as what you're used to—Max tells me you have a number of staff—but I hope you'll forgive me. Never did like strangers traipsing through my house. Had a maid come by once a week or so when my husband was alive, but only because he insisted upon lightening my load. You know, that's the problem with people these days." She didn't elaborate on the point but instead changed the subject.

"By the way, Max dear, I hope you two don't mind, but I've invited two of the neighbors over to join us."

"The neighbor who you think is going to murder his wife?" Max asked, an edge to his voice. "This is my day off, Mother, and those have been scarce as hen's teeth lately, as you well know. I do hope you didn't invite me over here to work."

"Don't be silly. I didn't invite you over to do anything other than enjoy a nice brunch. I did, however, think your lady sleuth might be interested in the goings-on next door. What do you say, Rosemary? Fancy a dive into the mind of a potential murderer?"

Taken aback by the question, Rosemary wondered if Ariadne's opinion of her hinged upon the answer, and so she made a concerted effort to keep her face from displaying the surprise she felt.

"I'd be happy to oblige," she said, and winked at Max when he grimaced and frowned his disapproval.

"I don't understand why you've got your hackles up over the man next door. I called over the fence to him once or twice while I was getting the place in order for you, and he seemed a nice enough chap to me. What grievous fault has he exhibited to make you think he's out to murder his wife?" Max's tone indicated it wasn't the first time he'd made the inquiry nor had he received a satisfactory response.

Ariadne huffed and continued puttering about. "When you've been around as long as I have, you learn to notice the little things. You begin to trust your instincts, and mine tell me he's hiding something. His behavior reminds me of old Mr. Millner back in the village. That one had everyone fooled, he did, except for me."

Her tone darkening, Ariadne told her tale to Rosemary while Max looked away. It seemed he'd heard the story before.

"When they found his wife's body sprawled on the flag-stones, he told the constable she'd tripped over her own feet and fallen through the window. Well, I knew that for a lie."

Fascinated, Rosemary wanted to hear more. "How could you possibly know?"

Ariadne's eyes sparkled as she pronounced, "Why, Annie Millner had very few talents in life, but she was nimble as a fairy, wasn't she? Well, of course, he'd pushed her, and do you want to know why? When he finally admitted the deed, he allowed as she had served leg of lamb one too many times. Didn't matter it was his favorite meal, and one of the few the poor woman could manage to cook to his liking. Cool as a cucumber was Mr. Millner." Ariadne shivered. "Mr. Joseph gives me the exact same feeling, like he's teetering on the edge and could snap at any moment!"

"You're being quite dramatic, Mother," Max said dryly. "You can't condemn a man simply because he reminds you of a murderer."

"I can do whatever I like, Max. Haven't you, yourself, said that to catch a criminal, you need only to see him clearly?"

Rosemary had heard the exact same adage from her late husband and when Max's face reddened ever so slightly, she assumed he had done the same.

EIGHT

When the bell chimed a few moments later, Mrs. Whittington shooed Max away from answering the door and forced him into a dining room chair. "Best not be you who greets them, lest we scare the man off. And perhaps for today, you're not a detective inspector. Today you're a banker with Lloyd's, because that's what I told them you do for a living." Without a second glance at her son's stormy expression, she hurried—or what accounted for hurrying, anyway—to greet her guests. Duke followed her out excitedly, ignoring Ariadne's commands to sit and stay.

"Sometimes that woman makes me want to spit nails," Max said while she was out of the room.

"I think she's absolutely fabulous!" Rosemary replied happily as she held back a comment regarding Max's suitability, or lack of such, for a job in banking. "In fact, I'm quite enjoying your discomfiture. It's a rare occasion to see Max Whittington flustered."

Max tried to maintain his irritated countenance, but Rosemary's smile was too much. "All right, I'll play my role. But I believe I'll take a page from the Vera Blackburn handbook and really commit to it."

It took a few more moments than expected for the trio to return to the dining room, and when they did, Rosemary quirked an eyebrow. The woman who trailed Ariadne appeared to be no more than thirty, but she walked with a careful slowness of someone twice her age and wore a thick grey dress more suited for winter than the summer heat. Rosemary wondered how she didn't sweat buckets in it.

Little Duke, whose barks could be heard from the moment the door opened, continued to run back and forth in front of the husband, baring his teeth at the man and growling.

"Duke, for heaven's sake, quiet down," Ariadne commanded, but to no avail. Even though the bulldog wasn't nearly as menacing as he thought himself to be, the new guests appeared somewhat unnerved. Finally, Max rose, picked the dog up, and unceremoniously deposited him in the back garden where he finally quieted.

Ariadne scowled and apologized. "I'm terribly sorry about Duke. He can be quite obnoxious around new people. I've got a man coming to fix that hole in the fence he keeps using to sneak into your garden."

"Slowly now, Dolly." The husband ignored Ariadne's apology and placed a protective hand on his wife's arm while he helped her into a chair. "You don't want to fall and make things worse."

Dolly's face pinked, and she murmured, "I'm quite all right. Let's not make a fuss." She settled into the proffered chair and then looked expectantly at Max and Rosemary.

"This is my son, Max, and his friend, Rosemary Lillywhite," Ariadne made the introductions. "Meet Cliff and Dolly Joseph."

Ginger-haired with a light spatter of freckles across her nose, and pale as porcelain, Dolly Joseph wouldn't have looked out of place amid a shelf lined with Dresden figurines. Against her husband's dark and ruddy coloring, she seemed more fragile still.

"Lovely to meet you both," Dolly replied breathlessly, as though the walk from next door had been almost too taxing for her constitution. "Please excuse my husband. He's overly concerned about my health, but I'm quite all right." She repeated the sentiment with great emphasis, though whether attempting to convince herself or everyone else, Rosemary couldn't tell.

What she did observe was that Cliff watched over his wife as if he found it necessary to anticipate her every need. To the suspicious eye—of which Ariadne seemed possessed—his solicitous manner might be suggestive of sinister intent.

Barely a moment passed before Ariadne pierced Dolly with a look and, with the unabashed shamelessness that only elderly women possess, said, "What is it that ails you, Dolly?"

"Mother!" Max admonished and earned himself a quelling look. "It's not polite to pry."

"Anyone can see this young woman isn't well. I'm merely asking why." The matter settled in her mind, Ariadne turned back to Dolly. "Have you been to the doctor?"

Dolly smiled ruefully and attempted to make light of Ariadne's utter disregard for propriety, yet her hand trembled when she waved it dismissively.

"Oh, you know doctors. If you're a woman, and the diagnosis isn't obvious, they assume you've dissolved into some form of hysterics and simply prescribe a tonic. Tastes like plain old sugar water to me, frankly, but I keep taking it for fear if I don't they'll send some nurse out to spy on me. I can't stand strangers traipsing around my home, and all a nurse would do is hover around like a butterfly and drive me absolutely batty."

"I understand. In fact, I said something similar not too long before you arrived," Ariadne agreed.

Dolly picked up the silver tongs laid out for that purpose, and from the top tier of the tea tray, plucked a fat, red strawberry from its perch. As she did so, the hem of her dress sleeve slipped nearly to her elbow, revealing a large bruise in the center of her forearm. Quickly, she pulled the sleeve back down, but not before her face pinked with embarrassment. Rosemary watched Ariadne's eyes narrow and flick in the husband's direction, but if he'd noticed the incident, his expression never wavered.

"If you ever find yourself in need of assistance," Rosemary waited until Dolly looked up, "You have only to call out for Ariadne, and she will be more than happy to come to your aid."

Changing the subject, Dolly spoke to Ariadne, "You appear to be settling in quite nicely. How do you like your new home?"

"Oh, I'm adjusting." Risking propriety because she thought the woman could use some feeding up, Ariadne placed another strawberry on Dolly's plate. "I do enjoy being closer to my son. Have you family in London?"

Another impertinent question, and one that replaced the smile on Dolly's face with a hint of melancholy. "None."

To cover her gaffe, Ariadne prattled on, "This little cottage is a far cry from the country house where Max grew up, isn't it Max?"

Max nodded. "Certainly. However, it's more manageable now that you're getting on in years." The comment earned him a frown.

"Don't pick out my tombstone just yet, dear boy. I still have some good years in me, and don't you forget that it was here, not at home, that I hurt myself. Tripped into a big hole in the garden while I was weeding the rose beds."

"You know," Cliff said, "If you spread straw around the roots, you won't have as many weeds."

Ariadne's nose lifted, ever so slightly, into the air. "Yes, but straw holds moisture, leaving room for rot to creep in."

"Actually, during the dry summer months, straw can save you from the necessity of watering the plants every day. Look at my roses, they're beautiful specimens. No yellowing of the leaves, no wilting."

He gazed out the window in the direction of Ariadne's rose garden, a smug look on his face. The old woman refrained from retorting, and Rosemary had to hold back a grin knowing the effort it must have taken.

Dolly smiled at Rosemary and Max across the table. "I wouldn't know a hoe from a rake and I have the blackest of thumbs. I can't even keep a house plant alive. Cliff has begun to insist I don't touch them, for whenever I do, they end up dying."

"That large hemlock plant in your garden seems to be growing quite nicely. You do know it's poisonous?" Ariadne directed the question at Cliff, who seemed to take offense at the question and narrowed his eyes.

"Certainly. The study of botany falls well within the purview of chemistry," he retorted. "Before one can combine chemical elements one must learn to identify those basic compounds found in nature."

There was, Rosemary noted, nothing more tedious than the

fervor of a pedant when expounding upon a topic only he found interesting.

"You will find, should you be invited to take a closer look, that the plant to which you refer is more commonly known as bishop's lace, which, to the untrained eye, is often mistaken for poison hemlock."

Ariadne gave him a look so caustic it could eat through a steel plate but again refrained, with effort, from making a fuss.

"What about you, Max?" Cliff turned his attention away from Ariadne. "Are you possessed of green fingers, or do you spend all your time in an office? I understand you're in the banking business."

Max's chest puffed out slightly as he prepared to play his role. "No, I'm afraid I'm not much for gardening. I'm kept quite busy at work, of course, with the exchange rates being in such a state of flux."

He waxed on for a while, making Rosemary wonder if he knew anything at all about the economy, or if he was merely making up facts. Either way, despite his earlier misgivings, he appeared to enjoy the ruse, and his mother's tightly pursed lips seemed only to encourage him.

"Yes, quite right," Cliff said vaguely, and then turned to his wife. "You're looking peaked, dear. Why don't we get you home now so you can rest?"

There went another round of Dolly defending herself, but this time, her protests carried far less conviction, and she finally allowed herself to be convinced that brunch was over. "Very lovely to meet you, Rosemary," she said as she rose from the table. "Perhaps we'll meet again."

"That would be my pleasure," Rosemary said with a genuine smile.

"Well, what do you think?" Ariadne demanded as soon as she'd seen the Josephs out and returned to her seat at the table.

Max cleared his throat loudly and answered, "That poor chap seems like a doting husband." His words echoed Rosemary's earlier thought but without any of the misgivings she had begun to share with Ariadne. What would Max say if she offered up her doubts for his perusal?

Her ability to sidestep the fraught situation was curtailed when Ariadne waved away Max's comment. "I wasn't asking you. I'm already aware of the fact that you, my son, are no alarmist. However, you're also a darned fool sometimes."

"You're simply looking for a fire where there's not even a wisp of smoke," Max retorted, though he kept a modicum of respect in his tone. "I think you should turn your attention to making other friends amongst your new neighbors, and then you won't have time to indulge in this obsession with casting Cliff Joseph in the role of villain."

"One doesn't necessarily need to see the smoke," chided Ariadne. "Sometimes, the scent of petrol is all one needs to know a fire is about to break out."

Rosemary felt caught in the middle of their argument, and decided to remain diplomatic. "He did behave rather oddly and seems to be an excitable sort." She picked her words carefully, but not carefully enough to stop a quelling look from Max.

"However, he also appears to care deeply for Dolly, and who could blame him? She's perfectly lovely."

"Indeed." Ariadne narrowed her eyes at Rosemary who decided nothing she could say on the subject would placate both mother and son. With that cheery thought in her head, Rosemary fell silent and stayed that way until Max turned the topic to other things.

By the end of the visit, Rosemary still couldn't be certain she'd made any headway with Ariadne, but she'd done the best she could.

NINE

On Monday morning, Max called to ask Rosemary if she could come to the station for lunch. Even though it wasn't the most romantic of overtures, she appreciated that he'd taken what time he could to arrange the date.

"It's feast or famine, it seems," Rosemary said to Vera while she dressed. "I hadn't the opportunity to spend any time with Max since we got back from Pardington, and now it's three days in a row."

"Are you tiring of the detective inspector already, Rosie?" Vera asked, bemused.

Rosemary glowered at her friend. "No, of course not. Max is wonderful. He apologized for the awkward situation at the gallery—running into his old flame—and then wanted me to spend time with his mother. Any other woman would feel as though she'd been swept off her feet. I don't know why it makes me hesitant."

"That's just your brain trying to get in the way of your heart, Rosie. You feel guilty when you're happy, and miserable when you're sad. Let yourself live; it's what Andrew would want."

"You always do know how to get right to the center of a thing, don't you Vera?"

"It's one of my many gifts, Rosie dear."

When Wadsworth pulled the car up in front of the police station, it was to find Max standing outside smoking a cigarette, his shoulders hunched as if a great weight were settled upon them. When he turned toward her, his scowl bore out the theory.

"Rose, I'm so sorry but there's been a change of plans," he said when she stepped out. "Aurora Kingsley rang and asked me to come back to the gallery. There's been some sort of disturbance, from what I understand. There wasn't time to ring you before you left, but I was hoping you'd tag along and perhaps give me a lift across town? We can have lunch afterward."

"Of course," Rosemary replied automatically, though her stomach churned at the thought of having to return to the gallery and spend any more time with Aurora than necessary. "Get in," she said, and he did, giving Wadsworth the destination as they set off down the street.

"I'm terribly sorry, again, Rose," Max said.

She smiled brightly and assured him it was no bother. "What's happened?"

"I don't know," Max admitted. "She didn't give any specifics, but the constable who spoke to her said she sounded distressed. With any luck, we'll sort things out quickly and still have time for a bite to eat before I have to get back to the station." Rosemary rather thought her appetite had gone, and furthermore, that Max's optimism was misplaced.

Aurora met the pair at the gallery door, and though she wore a lovely sheath in a floral pattern and hadn't a hair out of place, her expression was grave. "Thank goodness you've come," she said as she ushered them inside.

"I hope you don't mind that I brought Rosemary along. We were just about to have lunch—" Max tried to explain.

She waved off his concern and said anxiously, "It's no bother."

"What seems to be the problem?" Max asked.

At that, Aurora's facade broke and she dissolved into tears. "It's Sidney. He's in trouble, I know it. All the money from opening night is missing, and the office has been torn to pieces. There was some sort of scuffle, and I can't find Sidney anywhere. None of his chums have seen him since the opening, and he hasn't been back to his flat. There is blood, Max," she wailed, flinging herself into his arms.

"Can you show me?" Max asked gently, extricating himself from her grip.

Aurora collected herself, rather sheepishly, and led them both up the stairs to a small office above the gallery. The room had definitely been ransacked, just as she'd described, papers were strewn everywhere and drawers had been emptied of their contents. Even the sofa had been shoved out of place.

On the left side of the room, a closet door hung slightly open. Inside, a bank of pigeonhole shelves stacked with files lined the walls and was the only part of the office that hadn't been disturbed. Blood pooled near the edge of the desk, trailing a line of droplets towards the door.

"There isn't enough blood here to suggest a fatal wound," Max noted. "If Mr. Mariott was, indeed, attacked, it looks as if he put up one hell of a fight."

"If only I'd looked out my window at just the right time, I

might have seen what happened to Sidney." Aurora pointed towards the window where Rosemary could see a wrought-iron shielded window across the narrow way. "I just know he's lying hurt somewhere, or maybe worse, he's dead."

Just then, Sadie came through the door to the office and stopped short when she caught sight of the group gathered inside. Her eyes grew wide, and then she seemed to gather herself, as much as a woman as perpetually nervous as she could.

"Oh, hello," Sadie said, "I didn't realize anyone else was here." She appeared unsure what to say next and instead surveyed the room before turning quizzical eyes on Aurora. "What's happened?" she asked, her hands working nervously.

Rosemary noticed her nails were bitten down to the quick and filed the fact away for later contemplation.

"Where have you been?" Aurora snapped. "I've been trying to ring you since yesterday with no answer."

Taken aback, Sadie stuttered, "It was my day off, Miss. I had...I was...It was my day off." By now, her voice had reached a level of shrillness that made Rosemary grimace.

"So you haven't heard from Sidney then?" Aurora demanded.

Sadie's cheeks pinked, and she retorted, "Of course not. Why would I know where he is? I haven't seen him since he stopped by yesterday evening to pick up the bank deposit from the opening—" she broke off and looked helplessly at Aurora, who opened her mouth to continue her incessant questioning.

At that, Max stepped in, waving a hand to hush Aurora. "Mr. Marriott picked up the deposit yesterday? Did you see him leave the building with it?"

Sadie looked back and forth between Max and Aurora as if unsure how to respond.

"Answer the question, Sadie," Aurora said in the same acerbic tone she'd used before.

"I didn't *see* him leave with it," Sadie finally admitted. "I saw him pull the money out of the safe, and when I left he was in here, counting it all and writing the amounts down in his book. What's all this about?"

"Mr. Mariott hasn't returned to his flat. He hasn't contacted Miss Kingsley, and it seems there was some sort of altercation here." Max indicated the bloodstain on the floor, reaching his arms out to indicate that Sadie shouldn't come any closer. "The money appears to have gone missing as well. Perhaps he slipped it into the deposit box at the bank?"

Sadie's eyes slid from Max to Aurora and back again, and she shook her head. "I wouldn't know, honestly."

"You didn't see anything suspicious that evening? Anyone out of place? Anything at all to indicate what might have happened here?" Max pressed.

"No," Sadie replied slowly, "but I didn't stick around for long. I'd only stopped by to retrieve a shawl I'd left behind after the opening."

"What about enemies?" Max continued firing questions at both women. "Is there anyone who might have wanted to harm Mr. Mariott?"

Aurora waffled once again, and retorted, "Of course not! Everyone loves Sidney."

Rosemary stepped in then, both to diffuse the rising tension and to point out something she remembered from the gallery opening.

"I'm not certain that's entirely true. I witnessed an altercation between Sidney and Reno Riley and another between Sidney and Arthur Banks. It didn't appear as though either of them much cared for the man. Now, I can't see Arthur Banks as the type to initiate a scuffle, but Reno is another story altogether."

"Reno is all bark and no bite." Aurora brushed off Rosemary's concern. "He's got too much tied up with this gallery to get on Sidney's bad side. He'd never show another piece in London ever again. It had to be someone else. Maybe one of those protesters or one of the guests who attended the opening."

"Perhaps," Max mused. "Or perhaps it was nobody at all."

TEN

"What do you mean?" Aurora demanded.

Max remained calm despite her shrill tone, but it took a concerted effort. "Well, to be perfectly frank, I'm not even positive there was a crime committed here. If the deposit made it to the bank, it would mean Mr. Mariott likely left of his own volition. He could have been searching for something, and the blood could have been caused by an accident. Perhaps he left, dropped the money in the night deposit, and then went to the hospital. He hasn't been gone long enough for me to file a missing person report, but I can make some calls and see if I can track him down. It seems to me that if someone were going to break in and steal something, it would be the most expensive item in the gallery: the Renoir."

"That depends," Rosemary said slowly. "The average thief might not necessarily know what to do with a stolen Renoir. Such sales usually are made through a fence and then to a buyer who has, shall we say, a lack of scruples. Cash, on the other hand, wouldn't require any further legwork."

Max considered Rosemary's point and nodded once, then turned to Aurora. "Was the door to the gallery locked when you discovered this mess?"

"Yes," she answered. "I had to unlock it with the key from outside."

"Hmm," Max murmured thoughtfully. "You have a key, Mr. Mariott has a key, and it sounds as though Miss Dawson has one as well. Assuming there are no other copies out there"—he glanced at Aurora, who shook her head no—"Sidney must have locked it on his way out, suggesting he *did* walk out, unharmed. As I've said before, I don't know if there's been a crime committed at all."

Aurora looked around the office, and asked, "Then what about this mess? Obviously, someone has ransacked the place. Sidney wouldn't have done this himself."

"I can't know that for certain. There could be a logical explanation. Perhaps he tore the place apart searching for something he lost. I'll take your concerns into account, naturally, and I'll have one of my men check up on the deposit tomorrow when the banks reopen. For now, I'll take a look around and then we can discuss how to proceed. Give me a few minutes to examine the scene, and then I'll meet you downstairs."

Sadie's eyebrows shot to her hairline and Aurora looked as though she might argue the point but wisely nodded once and ushered the girl out into the corridor.

Nothing else on the upper floor appeared to have been disturbed. Even the studio space, situated across the corridor, was neat as a pin. It struck Rosemary as odd, given the temperamental nature of most artists, but then she remembered the state of her own studio and decided perhaps it wasn't that unusual to prefer a tidy workspace.

The confinement of damage to one area lent some credence to Aurora's theory, but Rosemary couldn't help thinking the most obvious answer was usually the correct one, and since both Sidney and the money were gone, likely one took off with the other.

As she neared the stairwell, loud voices spilled out from the gallery space.

"Are you telling me the man has run off to keep from making good on his debts?"

"I—" Sadie began to speak, but was cut off.

"Sidney's whereabouts are not what's important here. He said he'd made some sales, and I expect to be paid as we agreed. I won't take no for an answer."

The grating sound of Reno Riley's voice echoed off the walls as Rosemary and Max descended the stairs into the gallery proper.

The girl took a step back from Reno and said, as firmly as she could, "I'm sorry, Mr. Riley, but even if I had access to the funds—which I do not—I see here that only three of your pieces were sold." She gave him a total minus the gallery fee, then gulped audibly when his face went red and his eyebrows narrowed menacingly.

"That's not the deal I had with Sidney," Reno growled. "He owes me for every item in this gallery. That's what we agreed upon!" He took another step towards Sadie, who mimicked the movement backwards and then glanced around her as if looking for an escape route.

"Reno," Aurora interrupted, approaching the confrontation, her heels clicking across the floor and irritation evident in her voice. "I'm sorry, but whatever deal you had with Sidney is between the two of you. Since he's not here right now, you'll simply have to wait until he returns. Furthermore, I don't believe he *ran off* to anywhere, and the first priority is finding him. I'm sure you'll understand." Her tone brooked no argument, but its firmness didn't seem to register with Reno.

"I understand that I'm owed money, and now you're trying to get out of paying me," he retorted.

Not in the least intimidated by his anger, her nostrils flaring, Aurora took a step in Reno's direction in much the same fashion as he'd done with Sadie. "Your business is with Sidney, and he's not here right now," she repeated firmly. "I'm sure he'll settle up with you when he returns."

"My business is with the gallery, and I don't give a damn whether Sidney is here or not!" The man was beginning to become unglued, and Sadie, who now had her back pressed against the wall, watched the exchange with a terrified expression.

Max's brow quirked and his eyes narrowed. "That's quite enough," he said forcefully, pounding down the rest of the stairs to come to Aurora's aid. That he did so with great aplomb was irksome, but Rosemary told herself he was simply doing his job. "This is a police investigation now, and your attitude is an impediment to the process. I'm afraid I'll have to ask you to leave and not return until this is all sorted out."

"Thank you," Aurora said after Reno had stormed out. "But I could have handled him, you know. Like I said, his bark is worse than his bite." Her irritation with Max seemed to have evaporated, despite her insistence, and her eyes took on a starry-eyed quality when she gazed at him.

"So you said," Max replied without emotion. In fact, he appeared irritated at the display and supremely uncomfortable with Rosemary having witnessed it. "Now, I'm going to have to look into things, which means, Rose, that I'll have to beg off lunch today. I'm terribly sorry."

Rosemary had seen it coming, and she'd been correct in her estimation that her appetite had flown, so she wasn't upset about that. She did not, however, relish the idea of Max staying behind with a woman who stared at him adoringly, but there wasn't anything to be done about that.

"Of course," she said. "I'll leave you to your work. Perhaps we can do something later? Vera has a rehearsal this evening, so I'm free for dinner."

Max smiled and led her to the door. "I'd be delighted to join you. Believe me, I'd rather be anywhere than here right now."

"I would certainly hope so," Rosemary murmured. Once they were safely outside, she gave him a quick peck on the cheek and was off with one last backward glance at Aurora, who watched the exchange with an unfathomable expression.

Eleven

"Disappeared, you say?" Vera quickly swallowed a mouthful of cottage pie. "I can't say I'm surprised. It seems you're a magnet for trouble wherever you go, Rosie."

"This isn't my fault," Rosemary retorted. "Aurora thinks he's been hurt or killed, but without a body and the amount of blood at the scene, it isn't enough to suggest such a thing. More likely, the man simply walked away."

Frederick raised an eyebrow at that. "A man doesn't put that much money and that much work into opening a gallery, only to pick up and disappear without a trace. Particularly with a woman like Aurora at his beck and call."

"Is that so, Freddie?" Vera asked, a trace of irritation in her voice.

"Absolutely. She may not be the most classically beautiful woman in any room, but she's exotic and interesting. Everything a man like Sidney Marriott would find irresistible. Me, I like my women thoroughly English, with fiery tempers." He winked in Vera's direction, and she shook her head at him but softened.

"I barely met the man, but he struck me as off somehow, and I believe Max felt the same," Rosemary mused between bites. She continued to ponder the situation while Vera practiced her lines, thinking about the altercations between Sidney and Reno and Arthur the night of the opening.

Shortly after the commencement of dinner, Frederick had announced his desire to attend Vera's rehearsal that evening and pressed Rosemary into agreeing to accompany him to the event. His reasons, Rosemary had an inkling, had less to do with seeing Vera in action than his desire to ensure her co-star, Rod Stone, kept his eyes—and his hands—to himself.

"I suppose we'll get a chance to grill Max for more information. I'll invite him along tonight. I do hope that's all right with you, Vera."

"Of course, Rosie dear. The more the merrier. With any luck, the place will be packed come opening night, and it's always good to get unbiased criticism beforehand."

Being the dutiful suitor that he was, Frederick assured Vera any criticism of her performance was sure to come out in her favor. "No one on the stage will hold a candle to you."

"You've become dreadfully sappy of late." Rosemary's comment put a scowl on Frederick's face. "I do believe, Vera dear, that you've tamed poor Frederick into a shadow of his former, cheeky self."

Eyes narrowed, Frederick rose and left the table, ignoring the tinkling laughter that followed him from the room.

The Globe Theater was a hive of bustling activity with stagehands rushing to and fro and nervous actors and actresses pacing the space behind the stage while running lines and performing their rituals for getting into character.

"I'm surprised they let you back in here after what happened last time," Rosemary commented wryly to her friend.

Vera swatted Rosemary on the arm. "I'm working with a different director this time, thank my lucky stars. I do feel badly about punching Jennie Bryer during the run of *A Midsummer Night's Dream*, but she had it coming to her," Vera said, ignoring the fact that justifying her actions negated the apology. "Why don't you all take a seat and get ready for some real entertainment?" she suggested, having turned her attention away from her friends and to her craft.

The play, a romantic tragedy that owed much to Romeo and Juliet and was set in modern times, was, in Rosemary's opinion, quite well written. Vera's performance nearly brought tears to her eyes, but it was Rod Stone who stole the stage. A mere sentence into his first-act monologue, the entire room went silent, everyone's attention fully captured. The man embodied his character, every nuance effortless and somehow intentional at the same time.

It was easy to see how Daisy had fallen under his spell, and she wasn't the only one. Every woman in the cast and crew stared at Rod with a gleam of interest in her eyes. Frederick glared at him with unabashed hatred, his own eyes narrowing every time Rod and Vera interacted.

When the director announced that rehearsal was over and the lights came up, Frederick's face was stony.

"It's just her work, Fred," Rosemary said, laying a hand on his arm. "It's acting, nothing more."

Her brother brushed her off, mumbling an "I know," and stalked over to wait for Vera by the edge of the stage.

"Should I prepare to break up a fight?" Max asked when Frederick was out of earshot.

Rosemary waved a hand. "Probably not. Freddie tends to

flare up and then think the better of things. It's one of his more childish traits. However, if he isn't careful with his words, he'll be in for it. She's gone a bit soft on him since they started dating, but she'll revert back to the old Vera if he can't control his tongue."

"The old Vera?" Max wondered.

"She once spiked his gin with a laxative when he suggested her beau at the time was more interested in her financial assets than her physical ones."

"Well, let's hope we don't have a repeat of that. I think the play, despite Freddie's reservations, is quite good."

"Best change your review to 'spectacularly amazing,'" Rosemary suggested. "Perhaps the praise will put Vera into a high enough mood to overlook whatever gaffe my brother is likely to commit."

"How about that drink, Daisy?" Vera asked as the pair, along with Rod, exited the backstage area and approached Rosemary and the rest of the group. Frederick put a protective arm around Vera, but she wasn't paying any attention to him and didn't notice the glare he sent in Rod's direction.

"I wish I could," Daisy replied, "but I have a date with my easel and paints tonight. There's this piece I've been painting in my head all day, and I want to get it down on canvas while the idea is fresh. I'm sorry, but can we make it a date for another time?"

"Of course," Vera assured her. "I completely understand. Rosie here is the same way. When inspiration strikes, I can't drag her away from her studio."

Daisy pulled a lipstick out of her bag and reapplied a coat of cherry red to her lips. "If this one comes out as I've envisioned it, I'm going to send it over to the gallery for Sidney to appraise. One of the buyers from the other night indicated he'd enjoy seeing more of my work. Cross your fingers for me!"

Rosemary and Vera exchanged a look that stopped the girl in her tracks. "What?"

"You haven't heard, have you?" Vera asked. "Sidney has come up missing." Rod listened with interest, his eyes widening as Vera explained about the presumed robbery and the missing cash.

"Blood, did you say?" As if trying out a word he'd never said before, Rod repeated, "Blood. Blimey." He clicked his tongue against the roof of his mouth and shook his head slowly. "Blood."

Max gave Rod a sidelong look, then his eyes caught Rosemary's and widened slightly. She returned the look, added a shrug. Even Vera's lips twitched as she held back a smirk, then she turned her attention back to Daisy when that woman made a strangled, choking sound.

"Well, isn't that dandy," Daisy said, sinking onto the stage steps like a deflated balloon. "I suppose this means I'm out the money I need." Her hand fluttered to her mouth and her cheeks pinked. "What a selfish thing to say, and of course, I hope Sidney wasn't hurt, or worse. I was angry with him for replacing my pieces with Reno's, but I got the impression he would have made another choice if he could have."

Rosemary's eyebrow quirked. "What makes you say that?" she asked.

Daisy considered. "I'm not certain, just the way he broke the news, I suppose. Gentler than one might expect when essentially getting the sack. I assumed it had something to do with Aurora, though I've no proof of that either. She doesn't care for me, you know," Daisy added when the mention of Aurora set Rosemary's eyebrows off for a second time. "I rather think she despises other women, and she's quite possessive."

"I did get the feeling she enjoys being the only woman in the room," Vera agreed.

Max's brow furrowed, but he didn't say anything, and so Rosemary spoke up. "Surely a professional gallery owner like Mr. Mariott wouldn't let his fiancée's insecurities stand in the way of his business success?"

"Perhaps not, but I got the impression she's more involved in the business than either of them let on. She's the one who has the last word between them even if she feigns deference to him in public—in personal matters and business would be my guess. Let's just say, her feelings about me are mutual."

Rosemary thought she quite liked Daisy for her opinion, and then immediately regretted the unkind notion. It wasn't as though Max was interested in Aurora, so she had no reason to dislike the woman. Furthermore, when she looked over at Frederick, staring at Rod Stone with barely-concealed hatred in his eyes, Rosemary decided to give Aurora a break lest she end up resembling her brother.

Vera followed Rosemary's gaze and finally noticed Frederick's stormy mood. She sighed, grabbed his hand, and pulled him over to Rod and introduced the two men. "Rod, this is Frederick. Freddie, meet Rod Stone."

"Hello. Vera talks about you all the time. It's nice to put a face to the name," Rod said politely, giving Frederick no choice but to return the kind greeting. Rosemary snickered to herself, thinking it was probably killing her brother that Rod seemed like a nice guy just as Vera had promised.

Given the man's blank expression and the fact that his shirt buttons were off a hole, the collar resting unevenly around his neck as a result, Rosemary didn't think Frederick had anything to worry about.

TWELVE

"Vera!" Rosemary had to speak twice while Vera's fingers absently tore a piece of hot buttered toast into shreds that littered a rose-sprigged plate. "You seem distracted. Has my brother done something which requires some form of elaborate punishment?

Sighing, Vera dropped the crust back onto her plate. She had yet to dress for the day, and wore a robe over her nightgown, which she tucked beneath her legs as she shifted in her seat.

"Your brother has been perfectly lovely of late, save for his irritation with my co-star yesterday evening, but we moved past that well enough. I am disappointed that he had to return to Pardington with your father this morning, but I suppose work can't be helped. He'll be back for a business meeting in a couple of days, and I'll probably be more productive now that he's gone."

"Then why are you destroying perfectly edible baked goods?" Rosemary wanted to know.

Vera's pushed the plate away and sighed. "It's the play. There's something missing from my performance. Some nuance I haven't been able to put my finger on. I suppose I simply need a distraction."

"Then I have the perfect solution. Why don't you come with me for a visit to Max's mother? I think you'll find her an interesting study."

"All right then," she agreed, rising from the table and scurrying upstairs to make herself presentable.

Vera had nearly as much praise for the outside of Ariadne Whittington's house as Rosemary had. "It doesn't quite seem as though it belongs on this street, does it?"

"No," Rosemary murmured in agreement. "It looks like it should be sitting at the edge of a woodland stream, smoke puffing from the chimney."

"Complete with an old, witchy-looking woman picking herbs from her garden. Does Mrs. Whittington fit the bill?"

Rosemary swatted at her friend. "No, not at all. You'll see." She knocked on the door, waited for Duke's bark and Ariadne's command to come inside, and then stepped out of the way so Vera could take the full brunt of the little dog's excitement.

"Whoa, little guy," Vera said with a laugh, unable to resist the pup any more than Rosemary could.

"Hello, Duke," she said, and then ushered both Vera and the dog inside.

When they finally located Ariadne, she didn't resemble a woman with full control of her faculties despite the assurance Rosemary had given Vera. Upon the tip of her nose perched a pair of glasses with thick lenses, her silver hair was mussed—a floppy sun hat lay discarded at her side—and she was watching the house next door like a hawk. She hushed the women before Rosemary could say anything, and finished scribbling something on a pad of paper before greeting them.

"Come, sit," she said without any explanation. They complied, the scent of Ariadne's homemade hand salve—heavy on mint and eucalyptus—wafting over to open Rosemary's sinuses.

Introductions and pleasantries passed between the women, and then Rosemary asked, against her better judgment, what Max's mother had been doing when they arrived.

"I'm getting the lay of the land, so to speak. The first rule of subterfuge is to know one's opponent."

Vera peered at Rosemary, raised an eyebrow, and then turned to face the direction upon which Ariadne's gaze had been fixed. From the vantage point of the veranda, and owing to the angle at which the two houses were situated, they had a perfect view of Cliff and Dolly Joseph's front door in addition to that of the windows lining the side of the house. Both side and rear gardens butted up against one another, giving each an unobstructed view of the others' garden. "If only I'd known you needed them, I have a lovely pair of opera glasses."

"Why do you think I'm wearing these bottle-bottom lenses, child? My eyesight's as good as yours without them," the old woman replied with a wink.

With that, a friendship was born, and Vera's expression turned to one of amusement-laced interest. "What exactly are we looking for?"

"Anything incriminating, first and foremost," Ariadne replied. "However, what I'd really like to get a handle on is Cliff's timetable. I've been trying to invite Dolly over here for another tea, but he's insistent that she's too ill to go out or receive visitors. He's been quite cold towards me since the brunch, and I'd like to know why. When he leaves, I intend to march over there and make that girl tell me if she's in danger."

"I see where Max gets his desire to investigate," Vera said with a smile. "He and Rosemary are a perfect match. She can't seem to let sleeping dogs lie, either."

Ariadne raised an eyebrow at Rosemary, and said, "I have heard about her exploits, certainly, though I have yet to see her in action." She refrained from commenting on Vera's perfect-match comment, a fact which did not go unnoticed by Rosemary.

What had the woman expected her to do? Jump on Cliff Joseph, wrestle him to the ground, and force a confession from him?

With a wink, Vera pressed, "She's an improvement over that Aurora Kingsley we met at the gallery opening a few nights ago."

Rosemary felt as if poised on a ledge as she waited for Ariadne's answer. When it came, however, it was noncommittal and did nothing to relieve the tension.

"There was a time when Max was quite taken with Aurora's attributes," she said.

Vera might have pressed for more, but Ariadne sprang up to catch the water before it boiled, and the opportunity was lost.

A little while later, after the teapot rang empty, the cakes had been polished off, and Vera brought up to speed, Cliff exited his house, got into his car, and pulled away.

"I wonder where he's off to now?" Ariadne mused, jotting down a note on her ever-present pad of paper. "Not that it matters, for here is our chance to speak with Dolly without her husband listening intently to every word."

She made a move to get up from the table, but Rosemary made a decision, rose from her seat, and flicked her hair out of her face.

"I think, perhaps, I rather liked Dolly Joseph. I believe I'd like to check in on her and possibly bring her something to help lift the doldrums. Might you have something lying about that would fit the bill?" She asked Ariadne, whose lips curled into a grin that showed how pretty a young woman she must have been. Pretty, and full of fire.

"Why, yes dear, I believe I have just the thing," Ariadne said. "In my kitchen, you will find a whole cupboard full of my special jams. Even Cliff the gardener won't be able to top my brambleberry!"

Her enthusiasm allowed Rosemary to take a full breath for the first time since meeting the woman. It seemed she had passed some sort of test, only it was the last kind of answer she'd expected to have to give.

Twenty minutes later, Rosemary, carrying a basket full of jam and a fresh loaf of bread Ariadne had baked that morning, knocked on the neighbors' door just as, to her surprise, it opened. A drawn-looking Dolly gave a start and then said, "Oh, hello. Rosemary, was it?"

"Hello, Dolly. Mrs. Whittington—Ariadne—wanted me to stop over and check on you. Are you going out?"

"Just for a bit," Dolly replied. "I saw you all having tea through the window and thought perhaps I'd join you if it wasn't too much of an imposition. The sun looked so warm and lovely."

"It's not an imposition at all," Rosemary said, pleased to

have had an opportunity dropped into her lap rather than having had to finagle her way into the house under false pretenses. Dolly took the basket gratefully, making a fuss over the jar of jam, and deposited it back inside before following Rosemary across the lawn.

THIRTEEN

Ariadne played the gracious hostess while Vera and Dolly tucked into a conversation that centered around Vera's career on the stage. "I simply can't imagine putting myself out there like that, for all the world to see. You're a brave woman," Dolly said while absently patting Duke's waiting head. It seemed it had only been Cliff to whom the little dog had taken a dislike.

"Well, it's the stage rather than the screen, so it's not quite the whole world. Just a few bored Londoners, usually," Vera replied modestly. "I could get you tickets to my upcoming show if you're feeling up to an evening out."

Dolly blanched at the mention of her illness. "My health has been the subject of far too much talk. My husband worries so," she replied wryly. "He coddles me terribly, but it's not as bad as all that. I'm on the road to recovery." She sounded hopeful and made Rosemary wonder if things were worse or better than Dolly described.

"Of course you are, dear," Ariadne said, coming back to the table with a tray full of cakes. Rosemary hardly thought she could stand to eat any more, she was already so stuffed, but took one anyway and set it on the plate in front of her. "It sounds as though Cliff is the same as my Max. The boy is my pride and joy, but sometimes he looks at me with such pity I'd like to slap the expression right off his face."

With a tinkling laugh that lit up her face, Dolly agreed. "I understand the sentiment. It's always *drink this tea* or *take your medicine*. What he doesn't understand is that I feel better without any of those things."

Her hand shook slightly as she sipped the tea Ariadne poured, and then Dolly smiled again, appreciatively this time. "This is a lovely blend. Far better than the one Cliff makes. It's full of roots and berries he says will help me heal, but it tastes like bitter swill. He won't even let me use a lump of sugar, though I fancy my spoon would need to stand straight up in my cup to make the stuff palatable."

"I noticed a bruise on your arm the last time you were here. Is that part of the illness?" Ariadne asked boldly, apparently unconcerned that to most people her question would appear inappropriate.

Dolly's face pinked, and she smiled ruefully. "No, I'm afraid not. It's simply that I'm quite clumsy. No grace whatsoever, Cliff always says."

Ariadne raised an eyebrow. "You're certain that's all it is?"

"Of course." Dolly defended herself, tossing a queer look in Rosemary's direction. "You don't think I'm being abused, do you?" She began to laugh, and then said, quite seriously, "Cliff doesn't have the stomach for that sort of thing, I assure you. He's a gentle man despite his gruff ways. In the four—I mean seven—years we've been married, he's never once raised his voice to me, though I do appreciate the concern."

With a nod, Ariadne patted Dolly's hand. "All right, dear,

of course we believe you. Just know that if you ever need anything, we're only a phone call—or a shout from your bedroom window—away."

The conversation scarcely had time to move on before Cliff's car pulled back into the drive and he got out looking positively furious. "Dolly! What are you thinking? You're supposed to be in bed, resting and recuperating. Not outside, petting dogs and catching a draft."

Duke barked out his retort to the comment while Rosemary watched the scene with bated breath.

"I'm perfectly fine, dear," Dolly said, exchanging a glance with Ariadne that seemed to say *here we go again*.

The man marched across the lawn, trampling a patch of flowers on his way, and veritably dragged his wife back to their home. Once she was inside, he turned and retraced his steps, then leaned over the verandah railing and spat, "Leave us alone. You seem to have no respect for the position you put her in, and I won't have you luring her out again for her to catch her death."

Seemingly unable to help herself, Ariadne said calmly, "You ought to give your wife more credit and listen to what she wants. It's her life, after all."

Cliff ignored the statement, turned on his heel, and nearly hollered, "Mind your own business," before retreating to his home and slamming the front door.

"Well, then. That was interesting, wasn't it?" Ariadne said, her eyes locked on the house next door even as she spoke.

The trio discussed Cliff's attitude until Max arrived a handful of minutes later. "What have you been doing? Staying out of trouble, I hope." He eyed his mother with suspicion.

"Oh, nothing much, dear. In fact, we hardly had to do anything at all, did we?" Ariadne looked like the cat who ate the cream. "And we've learned some interesting information. Perhaps you fared even better on your search into Clifford Joseph's past?" she suggested hopefully.

"Not exactly," Max hedged. "The man appears to be exactly who he says he is. Married seven years; teaches chemistry, no criminal record, pays his debts on time. He purchased the house next door just before marrying Dolly. He appears to be a completely normal man by all accounts. It may be time to give up the ghost, Mother."

"Nonsense!" she retorted. "I can't stop feeling as if there's something more to him. I'm surprised at you, Max. You're usually so keen to follow your own instincts, I can't imagine why you want to discount mine. Is it because I'm female, or simply that I must be too old to be in charge of all my faculties?"

Vera tried to suppress a grin. It seemed as if the one thing Ariadne Whittington loved more than salacious gossip was goading her son.

"Of course not. Really, Mother, you'll have Rosemary and Vera believing I'm some sort of beast by the time you're finished."

The woman merely smiled benignly and winked at her guests. "They know perfectly well what I mean," she said in response. "Dolly might not be afraid of Cliff, but some women are blind to their husbands' shortcomings until it's too late to do anything about it. Did you hear what she said about the tea? Cliff's tastes bitter—perhaps that's because he's slipping something into it. Furthermore, the story about the bruise on her arm doesn't ring true to me. How would one—even someone as clumsy as Dolly claims to be—end up with a bruise on the underside of her forearm? It looked more like a thumbprint if you ask me."

"You've been impertinent again, haven't you, Mother?" Max began to chide her. "You must stop asking Dolly questions of which the answers are none of your concern. Surely you must agree."

He turned to Rosemary who considered while Vera spoke up quickly, the difference exemplifying their personalities to a T.

"I agree with Ariadne," Vera said. "I don't like that man, and Dolly is hiding something—I'd bet my bank balance on it."

Max looked to Rosemary as though she might be the voice of reason.

"I think it's best to proceed with caution." Rosemary's attempt at diplomacy brought a frown from Ariadne and a sniff from Vera. "However, if there was even the suspicion Dolly was in danger, you must see we needed to act. Andrew used to say the best way to know if the apples are ripe is to shake the tree."

As if hearing the word compelled him to a response, Duke let out a chorus of barks before Ariadne could get him to settle.

"I'll admit you make a sensible argument," Max replied and Ariadne let out a pleased sound, her eyes shining with triumph that lasted only until Max continued. "Now that you've poked and pried and turned up nothing but more speculation, I must ask you to let the matter lie."

Taking great pains to smooth over her mutinous expression, Ariadne merely nodded her response.

"Now, is there anything else you need before I go?" Max asked. "Aurora asked me to stop in at the gallery. I'm on my way there next."

"Oh, we'll follow you," Vera replied before Rosemary had the chance. "Won't we, Rosie?"

FOURTEEN

"Max, thank goodness you've come." Aurora pounced on him the moment she saw his face. "I rang the station, but the constable wouldn't tell me anything. Please say you've found my Sidney!" She barely acknowledged Rosemary or Vera, but this time Rosemary didn't blame her. Sadie hovered nearby, her mouth set in a thin line.

"I'm sorry," Max said, "but I'm afraid there's no trace of him. I came by to let you know the money Miss Dawson said he was preparing for deposit never made it to the bank."

Aurora's shoulders slumped, and her eyebrows crinkled. "What do you think that means?"

Max and Rosemary exchanged a look that said they were both thinking the same thing and couldn't imagine how Aurora hadn't come to a similar conclusion.

Standing there, hands twisting against each other, her pale green dress an unflattering color against her skin and needing the touch of an iron, Aurora looked rather worse for wear. Rosemary chided herself for feeling somewhat uncharitably pleased given the trouble she'd taken with her own appearance that day.

"Has Mr. Mariott ever mentioned," Max hedged, "whether he has family nearby? Or friends that would ... put him up for a time?" The hesitation combined with an obvious substitution of terms finally clued Aurora to the implications.

"I thought we had an understanding on this, Max!" Aurora sputtered. "Why would you even suggest such a thing? My Sidney is a good man. An honest man. He did not abscond with the gallery money."

"You wouldn't be the first woman," Vera said as if speaking from experience, "to think her beau incapable of treachery, only to discover the truth when it's too late."

"Believe me, I've seen it all, and unfortunately this is a line of inquiry I can't ignore," Max said gently.

From where Rosemary stood, she could see the corner of the Renoir, but thought it might seem churlish to indulge her curiosity at the present moment.

"Not my Sidney," Aurora insisted. "He's out there somewhere. Probably hurt and alone."

"We haven't turned up a patient fitting his description who ended up in hospital during the time in question."

Aurora seemed cheered by that news, at least, but as Max continued, her demeanor changed again.

"He seems to have disappeared into thin air, along with the money. Tell me, if you know, what will happen to the gallery if he fails to return?"

Dropping her gaze, Aurora turned away from Max. "I suppose I'll have to pay the rental agent and make good on the sales as it's my name on the lease." Behind her, Sadie blanched. Rosemary thought back to Daisy's comment regarding Aurora's involvement in the gallery's business. The girl had been correct, it seemed, though perhaps it would have been more prudent for her to remain impartial.

"Aurora." Max said her name in a way that carried hints of both sympathy and condemnation for having been taken in by a scoundrel.

"Don't you dare feel sorry for me. I won't have it. And you're wrong about Sidney. He wouldn't leave me to shoulder the burden alone."

"What about the Renoir?" Vera mused. "If you're in dire financial strait, could you sell it? It must be worth a small fortune."

"The Renoir!" Aurora exclaimed. "Of course. If Sidney did, as you postulate, take the money and run, he'd have taken the Renoir to sell. Leaving it behind would be utter folly if he was the opportunist you're making him out to be." Her excitement turned quickly to misery. "He must be hurt, or dead, or being held against his will if he left it here!"

"If that's the case, the money is long gone," Max explained gently. "You may have to sell the painting after all."

"I'll do no such thing! Not until I know for certain what's happened to Sidney. That's supposed to be your job. Why aren't you looking for clues? Shouldn't you have a list of suspects by now?"

Max opened his mouth to reiterate, no doubt, his contention that no crime had been committed, but Rosemary cut him off.

"Have either of you," she asked, directing her question to both Aurora and Sadie, "seen anyone suspicious loitering about the premises? Before or after the incident?"

"You know," Sadie said thoughtfully, "that man from the opening—the protest leader, Chas Matthews—came back the next day and again yesterday. He wandered around outside and peeked through the windows. I don't know what he was after, but perhaps it was the money."

Rosemary remembered the look on Chas's face when he'd set eyes upon Sadie, and thought perhaps what he was after was another glance at the woman. Still, he'd been dead set on forcing Sidney's hand, and she couldn't deny this would be one way to go about it.

Still, she couldn't come up with a valid theory for why the man would abduct or harm Sidney after the art of which he disapproved had already been shown. Such actions had no more purpose than closing the barn door after the horses had escaped.

Despite Aurora's vigorous protest and based on the information at hand, the only person with a motive in Sidney's disappearance was the man himself.

Fifteen

With great deliberation and a certain amount of restraint to her strokes, Rosemary applied a brush laden with the palest shade of blue to canvas. A blue so pale it was almost white teased the impression of sunlight spilling across the figure's left arm. Satisfied with what she'd done, she stepped back to assess and to roll some of the tension from her shoulders.

"Let's take a break, shall we?" She said to Vera who had graciously agreed to pose for the painting.

"Gladly." Vera arched her back and stretched. "Who knew sitting still would seem like such work? I feel as if I've spent the last hour in hard slog."

As Rosemary tilted her head from side to side, her neck made cracking sounds to let her know she'd been at the work for long enough.

It wasn't, however, the pain in her neck or that Vera had become bored that made the final determination the painting was finished for the day. It was the car that pulled up and parked at Rosemary's front doorstep. She tugged off the smock protecting her dress and exclaimed, "Drat. They're early."

Evelyn Woolridge waved away the helpful hand of her husband and heaved herself out of the car and onto the pavement in front of Rosemary's townhouse. She brushed some—

likely imaginary—lint from the bodice of her blouse and finally allowed Rosemary's father to lead her towards the doorstep where her daughter stood waiting.

Wadsworth must, Rosemary surmised, have been peering out the window, because before she had extricated herself, he had descended the stairs poised to assist with whatever the woman required. The point he'd been attempting to make proved moot, however, when Bertram, the Woolridge's own butler, sidestepped Wadsworth's advances and heaved the boot of the car open to retrieve the set of cases Evelyn had packed.

"Mother, Father." Rosemary greeted her parents with a kiss on the cheek while Vera kept her greeting to a simple hello. "It's lovely to have you here in London, but I didn't realize you'd be staying overnight. I can have the guest bedroom made up for you if you like."

Cecil was the one to wave a hand now. "We aren't staying, dear. Your mother simply doesn't understand the concept of a day trip is all."

"You'll thank me when the car breaks down on the way back to Pardington and you've got a clean pair of drawers," Evelyn retorted, bringing a surprised grin to Rosemary's face.

She had wondered whether the events that had transpired at Woolridge House—e.g. finding a dead body in amongst the rose bushes and the subsequent investigation—would change her mother's attitude towards life, and it seemed that perhaps they had. Mentioning her husband's undergarments in polite society—even if *polite society* only consisted of her own daughter—was something the old Evelyn never would have done.

The change was quite pleasing for Rosemary, as she and her

mother had often been in direct opposition to one another, particularly regarding matters of manners and propriety.

Rosemary shook her head as she appraised her mother's outfit but said nothing. Dressed in a tweed skirt, silk blouse, and matching jacket, Evelyn was overdressed not only for summer but also for a trip to the shops. A day in London was a rare occurrence for Evelyn, who abhorred traveling and preferred to remain at Woolridge House except for the two weeks each year when Cecil hauled her out, forcefully, to go on holiday in the south of France.

"I don't know why I had to come along to watch your father pick out a new pocket watch," Evelyn said, "when the one he has is perfectly serviceable. To make matters worse, he insists he's seen just the thing at some new shop called Mason Jacob's. What kind of name is that for a shop, I ask you?"

There was, Rosemary thought, only one reason her father would be watch shopping at this particular time, and when she looked at him for confirmation, he gave her a wink and a nod. The pocket watch in question would be handed down to Frederick on his wedding day as it had come to Cecil on his. Rosemary barely remembered her paternal grandfather, but she knew the story, as it had been told to her many times before.

This shopping trip, therefore, carried with it a great deal of implication. Had Frederick confided in his father? Would there be a proposal soon? Or was Cecil merely anticipating that his son's intentions were serious? These were the questions with which Rosemary wanted to pelt her father. Instead, she asked one of her mother.

"I've heard Mason Jacob's is quite lovely, actually. Wouldn't you like to see what they have to offer? You might find a nice brooch." Rosemary tried to persuade her mother even though she had a feeling she already knew the answer to that question.

Evelyn balked. "Why would I go anywhere besides Parsons? They're an established concern and everything they carry is of the utmost quality and taste. I prefer classic styles, and so does your father."

As his wife made the pronouncement, Cecil quirked an eyebrow, but wisely chose not to contradict when she insisted, "There's nowhere better than Parsons, I assure you."

"She's right, you know, Rosie," Vera leapt to Evelyn's defense. It had taken quite a lot for the two to come to terms regarding Vera and Frederick's budding romance, and Rosemary suspected that Vera would argue the color of the sky if Evelyn said it was pink instead of blue. "Mason Jacob's has a reputation for knocking off the work of more reputable jewelers while using cheaper metals and gems to keep their prices low."

With the two other women in cahoots, both Rosemary and her father gave up the argument. It wasn't that she didn't enjoy spending time amid a wealth of sparkling jewels, it was more that Parsons reminded her of Andrew. Whenever they happened to walk past the window, they'd stop to goggle at the fine craftsmanship that went into every piece. Andrew had been more frugal than his means, choosing to live comfortably but not extravagantly.

After spending time with Ariadne who did nearly everything for herself, it had come to Rosemary's attention that it required a staff of five to care for herself alone. When it had been both she and Andrew living in the house, the number of staff made sense, but now, although Rosemary felt herself well-situated, she wondered if she shouldn't be more mindful.

Surely, her money could be better spent, invested for the future, or even given away in support of a good cause. Surely she could get by with less, and she had no doubt the house-keeper and cook could find other posts, especially with the glowing references she would certainly provide.

Having held out hope that Vera would move in to keep her company, Rosemary had put off making any changes to her staff, and in light of current events, she decided she would continue to do so for a while longer.

"You'll come along, Rosemary." Evelyn wasn't asking. "And you as well, Vera. We'll have tea after."

Vera had a rehearsal to attend, but she agreed to go and shop for as long as she was able.

Sixteen

"How may I be of service?" The clerk, his face looking florid above a starched collar, assessed the group and chose Evelyn as the person most likely to be in charge of making purchase decisions.

"I would like to see," Cecil said, disabusing the clerk of his former notion, "a selection of pocket watches."

"Nothing too fancy, mind you." Evelyn tossed in her opinion. "Gold. Not silver. Gold is more dignified."

"In silver filigree if you have them."

Rosemary exchanged a small smile with Vera as Cecil less-than-subtly asserted his dominance. Evelyn sniffed, and in a snit took herself off to peruse the selection of classic-style jewelry—Victorian-era brooches and the like. Still, she kept an eye on her husband as he chose a watch of which she did not approve.

"I'll see you later tonight, dear," Cecil said once he'd paid for his purchase. "My meeting is right around the corner. I'll walk, and meet you back at Rosemary's with Frederick later this afternoon." With that, he ignored her irritation at his choice and made his escape.

"Isn't this exquisite?" Rosemary drew Vera's attention towards a sterling silver hatpin in the shape of a stylized wing inset with diamante crystals.

"That," Vera pointed, "would look stunning pinned to your blue cloche with the leather band. Simply topping."

"It's too expensive. I can't justify it," Rosemary said to Vera, under her breath.

Vera waved away her concerns. "Rosie, you hardly ever buy anything for yourself."

"You seem to have forgotten the unnecessary shopping trip we made just a few days ago. Perhaps if I return one of the dresses and a pair of shoes ..."

"Live a little, my friend," Vera reiterated. "It isn't as though you can't afford it."

"That's hardly the point. One must be sound with one's investments, and a hatpin certainly doesn't count."

Vera took the pin from Rosemary and handed it back to the clerk. "Ring me up for this, the pearls with the rhinestone clasp in the shape of a feather, and matching earbobs. There, problem solved. Call the gift a token of my unending friendship," she said to Rosemary and then, leaving her friend no choice but to follow, marched towards the cash register.

Deciding it was better not to argue, Rosemary let her go. When Vera got something into her head, much like Rosemary herself, she wouldn't let go of it no matter what anyone said. She spotted her mother still loitering near the brooch display and decided to join her.

"Find anything you like?" she asked, noting the irritated expression on Evelyn's face before she could finish the sentence.

"Yes, actually. However, the sensible clerk has gone and that man," she said indicating a person to her left, "feels the need to handle every piece in the store." The man looked somewhat familiar to Rosemary as the other clerk, a younger woman with wide eyes hovered, to do his bidding.

"This one is perfect, and my mother will love it. Can you put it on my account?" he said silkily to the shopgirl, who let out an involuntary giggle.

Once she heard him speak, Rosemary's eyes widened and then narrowed as she recognized Reno Riley, the artist from the gallery who painted all those horrible nudes. He held a gold-and-diamond necklace in his hand, and from where she stood, Rosemary could tell the stones were good ones, not paste.

When the young clerk hesitated, Reno heaped flattery upon her head, pouring on his somewhat oily brand of charm, and ending with, "It's Mum's birthday. Help a fellow out, eh?"

"I'll have to check the book," she said. "It says here you've owe an outstanding balance in the amount of—" she looked around and, noticing she had something of an audience, continued in a low voice. A short conversation ensued.

Whatever Reno said evidently satisfied her, because after a few moments of apparent indecision, she nodded and said, "I can do it this once, but be sure to settle up with us by the end of the month. It's for your mother, you said?" The girl tilted her head, gave him a speculative look from beneath lowered lashes.

"It is. She's the only woman in my life." The conversation took on such a flirtatious nature that Evelyn appeared appalled.

"I don't think Parsons is what it used to be," she said under her breath to Rosemary. "I doubt I shall shop here again." By now, Vera had joined them and was watching the scene with avid interest.

"That's the artist from the gallery, isn't it?" she asked.

Evelyn made for the door and announced in no uncertain terms that it was time to go. Outside, she let her frustration show. "It's uncouth! Shop girls soliciting men for dates. What is the world coming to?"

Rosemary didn't bother to comment on the fact that the exchange she'd just witnessed was actually quite tame compared to some of the things she'd seen. The admission would just launch Evelyn into a diatribe about the depravity of city life, and since Rosemary could recite said diatribe almost word for word, it wasn't something she felt she ought to be forced to listen to for the hundredth time.

"Why don't we get some lunch?" Rosemary suggested instead. "There's a lovely little tearoom just around the corner."

Her mother agreed, and they set out on foot but got no farther than a block away from Parsons before Evelyn stopped short in front of the window of a pawnbroker. She let out an exclamation and nearly pressed her face to the glass in a quite non-Evelyn like gesture. "That's exactly like the brooch my grandmother used to wear. I can't believe someone would leave it in a place like this."

"Why don't you go in and see how much they want for it?" Vera suggested helpfully.

Evelyn shook her head. "I can't be seen in such an establishment."

"Seen by whom, Mother?" Rosemary scoffed. "There's nobody around, and even if there were, what difference does it make? You want the brooch, go get it!"

Evelyn deliberated, turned as though to walk away, turned back for another look at the brooch, and then finally made her decision. "All right. What's the harm?"

Inside, Evelyn gave the salesperson a good verbal flogging and finally talked him into a discount of thirty percent off the tag price. She sent a flicker of a satisfied smile in Rosemary's direction and waited for the item to be wrapped.

For the second time, Rosemary did a double-take when the doorbell jingled and in walked Reno Riley, carrying the parcel from his trip to Parsons. This time, just as the last, he didn't seem to recognize either her or Vera, though whether that was due to his absorption in his own business or the fact that they were dressed down for the daytime shopping trip, she couldn't be certain.

He pulled the necklace from its package and approached the man at the counter. "What will you give me for this?" he asked, an edge to his voice.

"This is a beautiful piece, but it's quite new. Wouldn't you rather return it to the store?" The clerk asked.

Reno waved away his suggestion. "I know what I want, just tell me how much you'll give me for it."

The clerk named an amount that came in at less than half of what Reno had paid for the necklace at Parsons, and a short argument ensued. Eventually, Reno got the man to raise his price by ten percent, took the money, and exited the shop. His face, as he passed by Rosemary, was stormy with the barest hint of satisfaction.

"What on earth do you suppose that was about?" Vera asked while Evelyn made her purchase.

Rosemary continued staring after him, and said thoughtfully, "I'm not certain, but my guess is that he needs the cash after the gallery was robbed."

Something told her there was more to the story, but she'd

have to wait and see what other information Max had uncovered before she could put the pieces into any order that made sense.

SEVENTEEN

That evening, Rosemary required much gin to turn the afternoon with her mother into a distant memory, and Vera needed even more after the grueling dress rehearsal she'd endured. Frederick had spent the day attending to business dealings, and appeared somewhat worse for wear, and when Max arrived it looked as though he'd been carrying the weight of the world on his shoulders. The first round went down like water, and by the time the second had been handed out everyone's mood had risen to a much more pleasant level.

"Perhaps another holiday is what we all need," Frederick suggested as he drained his glass.

"No!" Both Rosemary and Vera objected, both remembering the group's recent trip to Cyprus where they'd become involved in another murder investigation. Frederick threw up his hands in surrender and didn't press the matter.

The mention brought Rosemary's thoughts back to the present, and she turned to Max apologetically. "By the way, we saw Reno Riley on the high street today. It was the oddest thing. He convinced the Parsons' counter girl to extend his line of credit for a gold and diamond necklace, then turned in the piece for cash at the pawnbroker shop around the corner."

Max sat back in his chair and crossed his legs. "It's not so surprising, actually. I did some digging after his little scene at the gallery. Reno Riley is in way over his head. He's owed money to every loan shark in the city at one point or another. Always manages to get himself out of hot water just in the nick of time. His criminal record is clean, so there isn't much I can do."

"Maybe he did steal the money from the gallery," Vera suggested. "If he's so hard up."

Rosemary shook her head. "No, I think Aurora is right on that count. Reno wouldn't have come back to the gallery and demanded Sadie pay him had he been the one to steal it in the first place."

"Oh." Vera's face fell. "That's true."

"I'll put a tail on him, see if anything shakes up," Max said.

"Inspector Whittington, sir," Wadsworth said, entering the parlor with a stern expression on his face. "I'm terribly sorry to interrupt, but I've just received a call from Mrs. Whittington. She said your presence was required and then disconnected the line."

"Oh, bollocks," Max said, his words slurring together slightly. "I've become too comfortable and I suppose now I'll have to ask for a lift, Wadsworth. Do you mind?"

"Of course not, sir. I'll just pull the car around. She did request the presence of the mistress as well." At that, Max's eyes narrowed.

"More of this business with her neighbor, I suspect," he said, shaking his head and resigning himself to the task. "Well, Rose, what do you say?"

Rosemary had already begun to collect herself, resisting the urge to down the dregs of her glass. "I'm in," she said, glancing at Vera and Frederick.

"You're welcome to come along as well," Max said, noting Frederick's eager expression. "Though I suspect you'll be bored nearly to death."

"I doubt it, chap," Frederick replied. "From what I've heard, your mother is a pistol, and I'd like to be there when the shots ring out."

"Very well, we'll all pile in. If Mother has a problem with me showing up with a troupe, she shouldn't have called on me after nine in the evening."

When they all arrived, it was to find Ariadne at the kitchen window, a pair of binoculars raised to her eyes, looking into the Josephs' side garden. Rosemary wondered if she'd had them squirreled away somewhere or if she'd acquired them after Vera's comment during their last visit.

"Mother, what is it?" Max asked, sidestepping Duke's attempts to climb up his leg. He absently shook the little dog off and went to her side.

"It's Cliff. I think he's up to something and I need you to check on Dolly."

At Max's disbelieving look, she scowled and continued. "I saw him out by the hemlock, trimming leaves. What else could he be doing with it, especially if he's harvesting in secret, in the dead of night, unless he's trying to do away with his wife?"

"Are you even positive that *is* a poison hemlock plant, Mother?" Max wanted to know. "Cliff said it was bishop's lace. You could be worried about a patch of wild carrots."

"Those are no wild carrots, Max. I can't fathom why you would question me on something like this. Bishop's lace has hairy stems and a central flower, whereas hemlock stems are smooth with purple spots. Even in the dark, you can see the purple spots." She tried to force the binoculars into his hand, but Max resisted.

"Even if you're right, what he grows in his garden is his own business, Mother. Are there no other uses for hemlock besides poison? Does it not have any medicinal effects?" He asked the leading question purposely. It was obvious to everyone, including Ariadne, that he'd done his homework.

She glared at him and said, "Of course it has medicinal uses, but it's a very dangerous plant to play around with if you don't understand its effects! And it won't be only his business if he's going to use it to kill his wife! We owe it to Dolly to prevent her from being delivered to her doom if we possibly can."

"Her doom? Don't you think you're being a bit dramatic? Perhaps he's trying to help her, and your interfering is only going to muddle matters."

He seized the binoculars and led Ariadne to her chair. Rosemary picked them up and peered out the window before Max noticed what she was doing. By the time he turned around, Frederick and Vera had joined Rosemary, and were all gaping at the neighbor's house.

"See what you've done? Now everyone's in a tizzy," Max scolded his mother.

"You, boy," Ariadne said, ignoring her son and instead focusing her attention on Frederick. "I've yet to meet you, but I can guess from the resemblance you're Rosemary's brother and Vera's beau."

"That's correct, Mrs. Whittington," he said, crossing the room and taking her hand gently.

Ariadne repeated her request not to be referred to as Mrs. Whittington, nodded her approval at Frederick, and then returned to pleading with her son for his assistance.

"What would you like me to do?" Max wanted to know. "March over there and break down the door? With what cause? The doctor has seen Dolly, and he doesn't seem to think she's in any danger. Hemlock poisoning is quick-acting, isn't it? Cliff couldn't be dosing her with it over a long period of time. We must mind our own business until there's real evidence that the man has done something wrong."

"And if it's too late? He's a chemist, Max, you said so yourself. Perhaps he's concocted a way to slow the effects of the poison. Duke has been over there, digging around at that plant for days. He's trying to tell me something. Dogs are far brighter than people give them credit for, you know."

Even to Rosemary, who didn't much care for Cliff either, the facts spoke for themselves. She thought perhaps loneliness was one reason for Ariadne's current state of agitation and vowed to visit more often.

Apparently, the same thought had occurred to Max, because he became stern and said, "I'm worried about you, Mother. I'd rather not have this conversation in front of people who are, to you at least, virtual strangers, but perhaps it's time to discuss getting you a live-in nurse. Someone to keep an eye on you."

Ariadne rose from her chair, up to her full height, and planted her index finger in Max's chest. "I don't care a fig who overhears this conversation. So much the better, as now I have witnesses to your insolence and disrespect. I'm your mother, I'm in perfectly good health, and I resent the assumption I'm in my dotage and in need of a nanny. What I need is someone to take me seriously and not behave as though I've lost my mind."

Max closed his eyes and appeared to be taking a quiet moment to collect himself while Rosemary sent an apologetic look in Frederick and Vera's direction. Neither appeared terribly uncomfortable with the display.

Based on his expression, Frederick found the interaction between Max and Ariadne fascinating and enlightening. It probably came as something of a surprise to realize he wasn't the only son dealing with a volatile mother.

Vera looked as though she were studying Ariadne with the curiosity of a student actress, and Rosemary wouldn't have been surprised to find that was indeed the case.

"Furthermore," Ariadne continued coyly, "I've been conversing with some of my new neighbors. You did say I should try and make friends, didn't you?"

"I did," he replied, "but I didn't mean for you to use it as another way to speculate about Cliff Joseph."

"Well, it matters not. What does matter is what the little birdies told me." Max looked at his mother as if he wondered whether *little birdies* was a euphemism or if she had taken to talking to the wildlife.

"Apparently, nobody knows much of anything about the Josephs because they've been antisocial ever since they bought the house. This street used to be filled with rental units, but the last few years have seen an influx of newlywed couples. It seems we got this house for a steal, Max, considering what needed to be done to the interior."

With her approval ringing in his ears, a hint of a smile threatened to show on Max's face.

"According to Mr. Potts across the street—he's lived here for years, and has quite a number of stories if you can get past the fact his eyesight is deplorable and he spends the majority of every conversation looking somewhere over your ear—"

Mystified, Max said, "Is there a point to this conversation?"

Ariadne lowered her voice for a more dramatic effect, "Mr. Potts said that Mrs. Joseph used to be a dancer."

Vera sucked in a breath with an audible whistling sound, and Rosemary slumped back in her seat to contemplate the ramifications of this new information. Max looked at Frederick, who shrugged as he had no more idea what had stirred the women up than Max, who finally had to ask, "What am I missing?"

"When we were here the other day," Rosemary said, "Dolly said her bruises came from being clumsy."

"Exactly right," Ariadne bounced in her chair. "Have you ever met a clumsy dancer? You mark my words, either that man is mishandling his wife, or she's suffering from muscle weakness which is a symptom of hemlock poisoning. Either way, it's damning evidence."

Vera harrumphed, then offered her opinion on the matter. "With my theater connections, I've known my fair share of dancers and I'm afraid your Mr. Potts is mistaken. Dolly is no dancer, she hasn't the build for it."

"How would you know?" scoffed Ariadne. "The way the woman dresses herself, it's impossible to tell what's under all those clothes."

Max's eyes closed for a moment while he collected his wits.

"I find this whole conversation tiresome. You're bored, Mother, and I understand that. Perhaps it's time to find a new hobby. I could bring you some books, or maybe you'd like to try your hand at needlepoint."

"Needlepoint! My goodness, Max, are you trying to send me to an early grave? Perhaps I should have been more worried about my own fate after all!"

When the telephone rang, Ariadne stopped mid-diatribe and stared at it with a quizzical expression. "Now, who could be calling here at this time of night?"

Her eyes darted to Max once she'd answered, and without a word, she motioned for him to take the receiver. "Hello?" he listened for a moment, and then his mouth set into a thin line.

"How did you get this number, Aurora?" he asked, his voice clipped. "I see, but I'm not on duty right now." He was quiet for another couple of seconds and then sighed. "Yes, I understand. Stay in your flat, and I'll be there as soon as I can."

"I've got to go, now. That was Aurora, calling to say she can see someone skulking around the gallery from the window of her flat across the street. I suspect she's been stationed there since Sidney's disappearance. Rose, why don't you have Wadsworth take you home, and I'll take Mother's car?"

Rosemary shook her head. "Absolutely not. We're all coming with you, and Wadsworth will drive." Max began to protest, but noticed the determined look on her face and decided there wasn't time for an argument.

"She's gone absolutely mad!" Max said when they'd all piled back into the car.

"Aurora?" Rosemary asked.

Max snorted. "Yes, but I was thinking of my mother."

"Oh, I think you're being too hard on her," Vera replied. "She's just feeling bereft in a new city and a new house."

"Nevertheless, I'm ordering that nurse. At least then, there will be someone to keep an eye on her when I'm not here."

Eighteen

"Go slow, but not too slow," Max advised Wadsworth as the loaded car pulled onto the gallery's street. I want to catch this guy and ask him some questions, not scare him away."

Wadsworth nodded once and said, "Certainly, sir. Discretion it is." He approached the corner and stopped, looking both ways as if watching for traffic even though there wasn't any to speak of.

"There!" Rosemary spotted a hooded figure walking along the cross street. The person was looking in towards the gallery windows, and then turned down the alley next to the building and disappeared.

"Let me out, then go around the block. Frederick, you trap him on the other side," Max instructed. Wadsworth replied with a stomp on the accelerator. He took two sharp right-hand turns and pulled to a stop on the other side of the alley, where Frederick hopped out of the car.

Vera glanced at Rosemary, and she wasn't surprised to see excitement shining on her friend's face. For once, it was an unwelcome sight.

"He could be armed, you know," she said, sobering Vera immediately.

"It's a good thing so am I," Wadsworth assured her, already halfway out of his seat.

They watched as the hooded man turned around and ran back in the direction he came. Max stepped out into the alley opening, the glow from the street lamps lighting him from behind and creating a formidable silhouette.

The man looked frantically in both directions and then, realizing he had no choice, raised his hands in surrender. Rosemary let out the breath she hadn't realized she'd been holding, but remained in the vehicle. Something in her peripheral vision caught her attention, and when she turned to look realized it was the top of Sadie's head poking up above the little window of the gallery's rear entrance.

Max and Frederick apprehended the lurker, with Wadsworth standing by as backup. When they turned the corner from the alleyway, his hood fell off to reveal his face. Rosemary wasn't at all surprised to find that it was Chas Matthews.

"Max, Sadie is inside," she said. "I think we ought to check on her."

His eyes flashed, and he nodded once. "Let's all go in where we can talk." He yanked, hard, on Chas's arm, and instructed Wadsworth to drive the ladies around to the front entrance.

"How did you know I was here?" Sadie asked once she'd unlocked the door and ushered the motley group into the gallery.

Rosemary quickly explained that Aurora had tracked Max down when she'd noticed Chas from her flat across the street. "She didn't say anything about you being here, however."

At that, Sadie blushed and chewed on one of her already

ragged cuticles but didn't respond and instead turned her attention to the interrogation.

"What are you doing skulking around?" Max demanded. He hadn't gone so far as to restrain the man, but he did pat him down and, not finding a weapon of any kind, determined he wasn't a threat. It didn't look to Rosemary as though Chas had any fight left in him, and she questioned whether he'd had much to begin with.

"I wasn't skulking," Chas explained. "I was keeping an eye on the place." His gaze never left Sadie's face, and his words rang true.

The bang of the front gallery doors startled everyone nearly out of their skin, and when Rosemary whirled around it was to see Aurora stalking towards them.

"What did you do with my Sidney?" She demanded of Chas, her voice rising almost to a shriek.

Chas seemed to wake up from his stupor and looked around for a way to escape. That he was more frightened of one woman than he was of two formidable men spoke volumes about Aurora's personality.

"Nothing," he stammered and hunched his shoulders as if to make himself a smaller target. "Nothing at all. I didn't do nothing to Sidney, I tell you."

When Max would have asked a question, Aurora cut him off, bent down, and put her face within inches of Chas'. "Then why have you been casing the gallery? Trying to get your hands on the Renoir?"

"Aurora!" Max's ears were bright red, and if looks could kill she would have been six feet under.

"What? If you're not going to ask questions, I will."

"I believe I'll take it from here," he said, taking her by the arm and pulling her away. She shook him off, but stepped back. "Technically, he hasn't done anything wrong that we know of." Max lowered his voice. "I shouldn't have taken him forcefully, and you could get me sacked if you don't stop this nonsense."

She flinched away from Max's harsh words. The high color of her face faded a little as they both took a moment to calm down, then she nodded. "I apologize. But you need to find out if he knows anything about Sidney."

"I'm aware of what I need to do, Aurora. Now let me do my job." He turned his attention back to Chas and said somewhat more gently than before, "Why did you feel the need to check up on the place?"

Chas looked to Sadie again, an apology in his eyes. "Because she's been here by herself, hasn't she? It's not safe."

"That's not true," Aurora cut in and received another quelling look from Max, which she duly ignored. "The gallery has been closed and the exhibit suspended. What would Sadie be doing here?"

Sadie rose from her chair and sighed. "I've been sleeping here, Aurora. I'm sorry I didn't tell you, but I couldn't make rent and I didn't have anywhere else to go."

All the anger drained out of Aurora, and she softened. "It's all right, Sadie. Why don't you come back to my flat with me, at least until we find Sidney."

With that decided, attention turned back to Chas. "Mr. Matthews, why do you think it's not safe here for Miss Dawson?" Max demanded, albeit more gently this time.

"Seen someone skulking around the place, didn't I? I don't

live far, and I walk these streets every night. I have trouble sleeping, and the walking helps."

Rosemary searched the man's face for signs of guile but saw none as he twisted his hat in his hands.

"Saw this fella dressed all in dark clothes, keeping himself in the shadows. I thought, maybe if he tried something, I'd be there to put a stop to it."

Max looked him straight in the eyes and said, "If you're telling the truth, your intentions are honorable. However, you've put yourself in danger in the process. What can you tell me about this man? Have you seen his face? Do you recognize him?"

"No, I haven't been able to get a good look at him. At first, I thought it might be Mr. Mariott, but he's not tall enough," Chas explained.

"Have you *seen* Mr. Mariott since the night of the gallery opening?"

Chas's eyes flicked to Sadie briefly and then landed on Aurora. "Yes," he admitted reluctantly. "It was the night after. I saw him leave. In a hurry he was, too."

It was new information, and its reveal left the room in stunned silence for a moment before Aurora erupted. She nearly lunged at Chas and had to be held back by an irate Max. "If you don't stop, I'll have you detained," he threatened, finally shushing the woman.

Rosemary was dumbfounded, and exchanged a look with her brother and Vera. All traces of the gin they'd consumed earlier in the evening were long gone, and she could feel a headache forming in her temple.

"Explain, please, and then you'll be free to go," Max implored Chas.

"Not much to explain," Chas replied. "Walked right out the front door, didn't he? Locked it behind him, and off he went."

"Was he alone?"

"Didn't see no one else with him, but he looked a little nervous. I noticed it took him a while to fit the key to the lock. His hands were shaking, and he swore a couple of times in the process."

"Did he have anything with him?" Max asked.

"A case, maybe. Under his coat, sort of like." Chas narrowed his eyes as he tried to remember. "It was too warm for a long coat, now I think on it. Probably why he carried it over his arm."

"Thank you," Max said. "You're free to go."

Still twisting his hat in his hands, and with his gaze fixed on Sadie, Chas said, "You won't be here alone, Miss?"

"Not anymore." Sadie blushed and looked away.

Once Chas had gone, Rosemary left Max to his business of berating Aurora and wandered over to the Renoir. Beneath the painting, the caption read, "Portrait of a Young Lady, ca. 1870's". She recognized the style of his earlier works, marveling at how a limited palette of colors could create such a juxtaposition of light and shadow. The subject, a rather plain-looking young lady indeed, came to life against the backdrop of the Seine River.

Before she had a chance to truly admire the piece, Aurora's voice rang through the empty space in an echo that jarred Rosemary from her reverie. She shook her head and reluctantly walked away from the painting, joining the rest of the group where they loitered near the center of the space.

"I already told you, I'm not selling it, and even if I were to entertain the possibility, it wouldn't be to Arthur Banks," Aurora said to Max, holding her ground. "Sidney will come back, I know he will."

It seemed an overly optimistic notion as far as Rosemary was concerned, but there was no arguing with Aurora.

"She's daft, I say," Frederick commented under his breath. "He's in the wind. It's probably Sidney skulking around, waiting to nab the painting out from under her nose. Now with that poor receptionist girl out of the way, well, here's his chance."

Rosemary thought perhaps her brother was correct. "Regardless, it's his gallery and his painting. I suppose Sidney can do whatever he likes with both, and perhaps now Max can wash his hands of this whole debacle."

She sincerely hoped that would be the case, but a sinking feeling in her stomach told her she wasn't yet free of Aurora Kingsley.

Nineteen

The Globe Theater was one of London's premier establishments, and that Vera had a chance to perform there again was something of a coup. She could barely contain her excitement as she tripped out of Rosemary's house several hours early with plans to stop off at her own flat for the remaining pieces of her wardrobe.

"I'll see you at the show," she said, depositing a kiss on her friend's cheek as she made her exit. "Wish me luck!"

"Break a leg, Vera dear," Rosemary called after her. She noted the sour expression on her brother's face and pierced him with a glare. "Be nice tonight. I know you don't care for her co-star, but I haven't seen Vera this excited about a role in a long time. The playwright has been touted as the next big star, and this could mean great things for Vera."

Frederick raised an eyebrow and went back to his drink without replying.

"Don't get too zozzled," Rosemary warned, to which he scowled and took another long sip. Foreboding rose up in her belly, but she tried her best to ignore it.

By the time she'd readied herself and met Abigail and Martin outside the townhouse, the worry had flown, and Frederick seemed to have swallowed his bad mood. She suspected it had gone down easily in a mix of gin and tonic, but vowed to, for once, stay out of his and Vera's business. Vera would deal with Frederick handily, and Rosemary preferred to enjoy the evening surrounded by her friends.

"Where is Max?" Abigail asked when she noticed it was only Rosemary and Frederick loitering on the doorstep.

"He's meeting us there," Rosemary explained. "Some pressing business down at the station has kept him tied to the place, but he promised to arrive before the show starts."

Abigail suggested Rosemary and Frederick go along with her and Martin, and they all piled in for the short drive to the theater. A fan of Vera's long before having met her in person, Abigail chatted about the play the entire way, her excitement reaching a crescendo as they pulled to a stop several blocks from the Globe.

Rosemary craned her neck to see above the crowd milling about near the entrance, looking for Max. "Do you see him anywhere?" she asked her brother, who stood nearly a foot taller than her, even though she was wearing heels.

"No," Frederick said after a quick scan. "He's probably inside. Let's go."

There was no sign of him in the lobby or at the bar, and he wasn't sitting in his designated seat when the foursome finally arrived at their row. Rosemary hoped that whatever had kept him so late wouldn't cause him to miss the play, and even more that it hadn't anything to do with the Mariott Gallery or Aurora Kingsley but had a sinking feeling that was probably the case.

"Stop shifting." Frederick nudged his sister with an elbow. "He'll be here when he can."

Just before the lights went down, Max finally arrived and had to awkwardly step in front of the entire row to get to his seat. "I'm sorry, Rose, I know I'm terribly late," he said apologetically.

"Is everything all right?" she asked, waving away his apology.

"Not exactly. Reno Riley managed to slip the tail I put on him. He's gone for now, and I had to have a conversation with the constable I'd assigned to him. It was not a pleasant one," he said, frowning. "Until Mr. Mariott turns up, the case is, unfortunately, ongoing."

Rosemary's brow furrowed, but she didn't have time to think any more about Reno's escape, and couldn't in any case because as the lights went down, Max took her hand in his and then the curtain rose.

A million thoughts raced through Rosemary's mind. That her fingers tingled against the heat of Max's hand. That she was never going to remember a single moment of the play at this rate.

But she did because the play was that good.

From the moment Vera delivered her first line, she commanded the stage with her presence, and it wasn't just the men who fell under her thrall.

"She's even better than her mother," a woman whispered from the row of seats behind them. Rosemary made a note to remember to tell Vera, then promptly forgot everything when the story being played out stole her breath away.

Dressed in flowing chiffon, Vera stood at the edge of the stage, her hands fisted at her sides, her face a mask of sadness.

The footlights picked out the lone tear that shone high on the blush of her cheek.

Whatever line she spoke, Rosemary barely registered the words so powerful was the emotion portrayed, and when Rod stepped into the light, reached for Vera, and spun her into his arms, every woman in the packed house inhaled. When he gazed down at her, then gently laid his lips over hers, the women all sighed.

Frederick snorted.

And then, he spent the rest of the play shifting in his seat and muttering under his breath.

Rosemary exchanged a glance with Max and decided the look on his face fell somewhere between resigned and amused.

"Well, that was entertaining." Frederick's tone sounded as if he'd been anything but amused. "I'm to meet Vera backstage."

"I am as well," Rosemary said to his disappearing back. "I'm sorry, Max."

"For what?"

"Oh, I don't know, but I'm certain there will be something before this is over." Smiling, she tucked her hand in Max's arm and the two made their way towards the stage.

"It was indecent." The dressing room door barely muffled Frederick's voice as Rosemary and Max approached. "The way he touched you. I won't have it."

"We could just go for a drink," Max suggested. "Let them sort it out on their own."

"Tempting. So very tempting." Yet, Rosemary pushed open the door if for no other reason than that Vera would never desert her in a time of need. Friendship required Rosemary return the favor.

Once inside, she tried to bore a hole through Frederick with a look, and when the ploy failed, Rosemary turned her attention to Vera and offered a hug.

"Darling, you were sensational. Simply marvelous. There wasn't a dry eye in the house for that last scene."

Vera preened, and then the worst happened. Rod appeared in the doorway.

Seeing him, Rosemary offered, "Congratulations on your performance. I predict the show will be a hit for weeks to come."

"Weeks?" Frederick burst out.

"Yes, of course." Vera looked at him as though he were daft. "You're aware of how these things work, are you not? A play runs for weeks, or sometimes months if ticket sales are good. The longer the play runs, the better. We're just barely into the season, so the initial run is three nights a week."

What good did it do, Rosemary asked herself, to try and defuse the situation when Vera was just as happy to touch a match to a powder keg?

"No," Frederick declared. "This will not do. It will not do at all. I won't have you kissing him three nights a week."

Things might have ended better if Rod hadn't chosen that moment to speak up. "Come now, old chap, you're acting as though I like kissing your girl."

Vera rounded on Rod, looked from him to Frederick, then back again as if to decide which man to address first. She settled on Rod. "Is there something about kissing me you find objectionable?"

"No. Not as such." Rod blushed. "It's just—" He shrugged, which didn't do anything to help his case.

"Well, you needn't worry," Frederick exclaimed, "you won't be required to endure Vera's kisses three nights a week because she won't be starring in any play with the likes of you."

"If we take two steps back, we can escape. They won't even notice we're gone," Max whispered in Rosemary's ear.

Vera reached down, pulled off her pump, and advanced upon Frederick with it as if she meant to do some serious harm. "I'll do as I like, Frederick Woolridge," her tone rising in pitch and volume as she approached him, "and you'd better think twice before you go making decisions for me!"

Frederick flinched and held up a hand to stave her off. "Put the shoe down, Vera."

But Vera was past the point of reasoning.

Abigail and Martin entered the scene just then, coming up behind Rosemary and Max and craning their necks to watch it all play out.

She got within several inches of him and jabbed her finger at him, her face mottled with anger. "I don't know what kind of woman you think I am, Frederick Woolridge, but I don't take my orders from you and I never will! If you can't accept that, the choice is yours."

She left the ultimatum hanging in the air, and Rosemary watched as her brother's face ran a gamut of emotions that ended in resigned anger.

"If that's how little my feelings mean to you, perhaps it's best I leave. I'll see you at home, Rose," he said with one last, long look at Vera.

Rosemary stepped aside, as did the rest, and allowed him to stalk out. She suspected the long walk back would calm his temper and knew better than to follow.

"I'm going for a drink with Daisy," Vera declared around the lump in her throat. "Rosie, Abigail, you're welcome to come along. The rest of you men can feel free to follow Frederick."

With that, she slammed the dressing room door, leaving her friends in stunned silence.

TWENTY

osemary had assured Max that she and the girls would call on Wadsworth for a lift back to the townhouse and shoved him off with Martin while she and Abigail dealt with Vera. Now, seated in a comfortable booth that looked out onto the bustling High Street, she'd wiped her tears and launched into a half-drunken diatribe against the opposite sex.

"He's mad if he thinks I'm going to give in to his every demand," Vera sputtered. "He knew who I was when we got involved. It shouldn't come as a surprise that I'm independent."

"At least you have a man to be angry with," Daisy lamented. "I've begun a rather unsuccessful relationship with one of my paintings, and though the subject is rather handsome, he's not at all responsive," she quipped.

Vera laughed in spite of herself. "I'm rather inclined to believe I might prefer talking to canvas than to Frederick at the moment."

"It's probably difficult for him to watch you kissing another man, although that's no excuse." Abigail hastened to add the last part when Vera pierced her with a glare.

Rosemary's lip quivered; she'd been keeping out of the conversation for just that reason. Vera was in no mood to entertain commentary that didn't agree with her current point of view, no matter how valid it might be.

Daisy took a sip of her drink, sat back in her seat, and crossed her legs. "Particularly a man who looks like Rod Stone. If he had any idea how dull the man actually is in real life, perhaps he'd have a different opinion."

"I take it the shine has worn off," Vera commented with a raised eyebrow.

"Oh, his finish is absolutely dull. He might be nice to look at, but I need more than that. Rod is married to his craft, anyway. I suppose I would be, too, if it were all I had going for me," Daisy replied. "That sounds terribly harsh; I think I've had too many drinks. Fancy a refill, anyone?" she asked with a grin.

Rosemary, seated closest to the edge of the booth and eager for an escape, rose and said, "I'll go get them. You three stay here, enjoy yourselves."

Her only contributions to the subject at hand would involve either Max, with whom she hadn't, as yet, had a true fight, or Andrew, whose memory she refused to sully by bringing up past grievances.

She approached the bar to place her order even though the waiter would have been more than obliged to do so and let out a breath of relief for the few minutes of reprieve from the conversation happening at the table.

"Be right with you," the barkeep barked, his attention on a man halfway down the bar with his head in his hands.

"Hey there, chap," the barkeep said sharply. "Are you all right?"

The man raised one bandage-covered hand, and after a moment, his head followed. Rosemary started and sucked in a breath. It was the hulking man from the gallery opening, and she dug back into her memory of that evening to produce his name. Fritz, she decided, remembering how he'd shoved Chas Matthews out the door after he'd pushed inside to rail at Sidney.

She debated whether or not to approach him and perhaps ask him a few questions, but the barkeep returned and asked for her order. By the time she'd asked for four G&Ts to be delivered to her table, Fritz was gone and Rosemary wondered if she'd missed a prime opportunity.

Reluctantly, she returned to her seat just in time to hear Daisy discussing whether or not she had decided to take Mr. Banks up on his offer to display her work in his gallery.

"Apparently, he's got a line on a Renoir painting too. He seemed to think it would sway my decision if I knew he could offer the same amount of exposure as the Mariott Gallery, and I think he might have been correct in that estimation. He's willing to display far more of my pieces than Sidney did, and he even offered an advance so I could pay for my mother's nurse. I suppose I should be thrilled."

While Abigail and Vera encouraged her to accept the offer, Rosemary was focused on one thing: how odd it was that not one, but two lost Renoir paintings had turned up in the course of a few weeks. The thought stayed with her until Vera stated, rather drunkenly, that she was ready to go.

Twenty-One

"Of course, Max. It would be my pleasure to spend some time with your mother," Rosemary said into the telephone receiver the next morning.

With a sigh, he replied, "Thank you. I want to make certain the nurse is working out, but I've got some paperwork to take care of. If I can tear myself away from my desk, I'll meet you at her house this afternoon. Try to keep her out of trouble."

"That sounds like a fool's errand to me, but I'll do my best."

"You're an angel, Rose," Max replied. "I'll call and let her know you'll be along shortly."

Duke's bark met Rosemary at the door, and this time she stepped inside without waiting for Ariadne's signal. Something about the little cottage and the woman who lived inside made her feel as though she were entering her own home, and the thought brought a smile to her face.

"Hello?" she called, sidestepping the pup after giving him a good scratch behind his ears. When she heard a commotion coming from the kitchen, she headed in that direction with Duke racing around her feet. When she arrived, she found Ariadne in a standoff with a stout, ornery looking woman in a nurse's uniform. Her hands were on her hips, and she looked as though at any second she might pull a pistol out of her belt.

"What could you possibly be thinking? You never pour the milk in before the tea. Is that how they do it in America or are you simply daft?"

Before the nurse could reply, Ariadne banished her to the bedroom, insisting the bedding be stripped and laundered immediately.

When she had disappeared, the sound of an engine roaring to life outside had Ariadne looking out the window. One eyebrow raised, and she turned to Rosemary with mischief in her eyes.

"Rosemary, why don't we sit out on the veranda while Miss Montgomery tends to the wash," Ariadne suggested with a wiggle of her eyebrows that let Rosemary know she was up to no good. Never one to argue with her elders, Rosemary complied and realized all too late just what Max's mother had in mind.

"Let's go," she said, handing Rosemary a set of car keys. "You can drive, can't you?"

"Of course I can drive," Rosemary replied, "though I don't think we ought to be running off. Won't the nurse call Max or the service when she realizes you're gone?"

Ariadne waved away Rosemary's concerns. "Pish posh. I'm not under house arrest, and we'll leave a note. We don't have long though, so hurry up."

She picked up her handbag and made her way outside with more spring in her step than Rosemary would have thought possible considering the state of her hip. Perhaps Max had been wrong and his mother didn't need round-the-clock supervision after all.

"See, he's just pulled away, and now we can follow him," Ariadne said, pointing to the car rushed past the end of the driveway.

"This is about Cliff Joseph again, isn't it?" Rosemary asked, having made no move to start the engine.

Ariadne sighed and rolled her eyes. "Yes, of course, dear. Now, let us be off, shall we, lest we lose him." It seemed as though the woman had no doubt Rosemary would follow her instructions and, unwilling to let her possible future mother-in-law down, she started the car and pulled out after Cliff.

He drove safely to the end of the street, turned right, and then gunned the engine, causing Rosemary to start. "Are you afraid of the accelerator?" Ariadne asked, looking positively gleeful at the thought of a chase.

Rosemary pressed her foot to the pedal, determined to neither disappoint Ariadne or lose Cliff as she avoided other automobiles and pedestrians. They followed, far enough behind not to be noticed, while he took turn after turn through the streets of London.

"Wherever do you think he's going?" Ariadne wondered at about the same time Rosemary was beginning to wonder the same thing.

The words had no more than left Ariadne's lips when Cliff stopped abruptly and parked in front of Bernardes Trading. When he exited the vehicle, he kept his head down and walked inside without stopping to take in his surroundings, and Rosemary was able to relax.

She chose a spot at a safe distance from Cliff's car where Ariadne's would be hidden behind a lorry dropping off supplies, but before she could get out and open the passenger door, Ariadne was already out and on her way towards the front of the shop.

"Now we'll see what he's all about, won't we?"

"Be careful, or he'll see us and know we followed him," Rosemary warned. "Why do you suppose he came all the way to this particular shop? There must have been at least one such establishment we passed along the way."

"That's precisely what we're going to find out. I told you he was hiding something," Ariadne retorted.

Rosemary shrugged and followed her, as there seemed no getting out of it and she'd already come this far.

Without looking left or right, Cliff made his way through the shop as if he knew exactly where to find what he wanted. In an out-of-the-way corner, he pawed through a small selection of thermometers, setting aside several with silver bulbs at the bottom.

While Rosemary and Ariadne peered around the corner to watch, Cliff's selection process took almost as long as it took Vera to choose a new hat. He shook the thermometers, tipped them this way and that, held them up to the light checking for whatever criteria he deemed fitting, and finally purchased the entire batch.

His steps as he left were far more sprightly than when he arrived, and he was already back in his automobile and pulling away from the curb when Rosemary and Ariadne exited the store.

"Curious, don't you think?" Ariadne repeated several times. "What does a man need with so many thermometers?"

"No idea." Rosemary shrugged and wondered how she would explain the excursion to Max.

Arriving back at the cottage, they discovered that buying the thermometer had not been Cliff's only errand, as he not only juggled the parcel from the hardware store, but he'd been to collect the post and also carried several letters as well. On the way inside, he dropped an envelope into the grass and, not having noticed his mistake, meandered down the path and into his house. Rosemary opened her mouth to call out to him as she exited the car, but Ariadne shushed her.

"Be quiet, girl, and don't look a gift horse in the mouth," she snapped, looking at Rosemary through narrowed eyes, her expression suggesting that perhaps Rosemary wasn't as clever as she thought.

Under the guise of pulling some weeds from her front beds, Ariadne scooped up the envelope just as Miss Montgomery opened the front door. "Where did you run off to?" she grumbled. "I've put in a call to the service and asked to be reassigned. Clearly, you don't find my presence necessary, and there are other patients who do."

She flounced back inside, and once she'd disappeared, Ariadne let loose the giggle she'd been holding in. "That was easy," she announced happily.

Inside, she sat down in her usual spot at the dining room table and began sorting through the mail. Before she had a chance to examine the letter Cliff had dropped, Duke's bark pierced the air. Rosemary realized, abruptly, that she hadn't been accosted by the little dog upon their entrance to the house.

Ariadne rose and stalked out the back door. "I'll get him," she said on her way.

While she was gone, Rosemary picked up the letter. It was addressed to Delores Joseph, and something about that struck Rosemary as odd. With a nickname like Dolly, she'd expected the woman's full name to be Dorothy, not Delores.

"Duke!" she heard Ariadne shout from the verandah. "Get back here, you rotten little beast!" His barks were punctuated by growls he considered menacing even though Rosemary doubted he could do much damage given the chance. When she looked out the window and saw that Duke had managed to find a way into the Josephs' rear garden and was digging around beneath his hemlock plant, she set the letter back down on the table and went outside to help.

By now, Cliff had emerged from his house and was stalking across the garden towards the dog. "I thought you said you were having the fence repaired," he shouted angrily.

"I do apologize," Ariadne said meekly, causing Rosemary to raise an eyebrow. The woman was playing nice, but there was a hardness in her eyes.

"If he comes over here again, I'm going to call the pound and have him collected. I mean it, keep him out of my garden." Cliff picked the dog up by the scruff of his neck, narrowly avoiding Duke's attempts to nip his fingers, and chucked him, unceremoniously, over the fence.

Rosemary's eyes widened, and she rushed down the short set of stairs to scoop the little dog into her arms. She examined his paws and, deciding he was no worse for wear, turned her attention to Cliff.

"One can judge the character of a man by the way he treats animals. You, sir, are a brute. Come on, Duke," Rosemary said, ushering Ariadne inside and slamming the door behind her.

"Well, I don't know if he's trying to kill his wife, but what I do know is that he's asking for trouble." She rummaged through the refrigerator and found a piece of leftover beef roast, slipping the dog a little treat and bringing a smile to Ariadne's face.

"He's quite taken with you," Ariadne said, watching Duke rub his head against Rosemary's calf.

She gave him one last pat and then sank into the chair opposite Ariadne. She didn't realize a morning with an octogenarian could be so tiring, but all she wanted to do now was go home, take a nice long nap, and forget Cliff Joseph existed.

Instead, she fixed a tea tray and sat down across from Ariadne. As soon as she raised the cup to her lips, two things happened at once. Miss Montgomery emerged from the guest bedroom having gathered her things, and Max came in through the front door.

"Good day, and good luck finding another nurse willing to deal with you and your obnoxious little dog!" she said as she sailed out of the house.

"Wait, what's happening?" Max asked, but she didn't pay him any mind, as she tottered down the path to where a car was waiting.

Max marched into the kitchen to find his mother sipping tea with a serene expression on her face. "Why did the nurse just walk out?"

"Because she was unnecessary in the first place, and it didn't take her long to realize it," Ariadne retorted.

"Mother," Max admonished, "now they'll have to send another."

The ensuing argument made clear Ariadne's opinion on the subject, and by the time it was over, Max had to return to the station, giving Rosemary no chance to tell him about the goings-on of the afternoon. She rather thought that turn of events might be for the best, though as she was beginning to see why his patience with his mother had thinned to a veritable sliver.

Twenty-Two

Vera having gone to a gathering of her theater crowd on Sunday morning, Rosemary found herself alone with Frederick. His behavior after the play hadn't yet been forgotten or forgiven, so Vera went alone. The slight hadn't gone unnoticed by Frederick, and he was in a rotten mood, pacing the floor in the dining room and muttering to himself while Rosemary tried to enjoy her breakfast.

"Will you please either sit down or find something else to do?" Rosemary finally demanded. "You're practically vibrating, I can feel it."

"You would be too, Rosie, if you were in my shoes."

"I'd never be in your shoes, dear brother," she deadpanned. "I'm not a jealous idiot."

Frederick glared at his sister and sat down at the table. "Get off your high horse, Rose. You don't like that Aurora woman any more than I like Rod Stone." The actor's name came out sounding like a slur.

"No, perhaps not, but I know when to keep my mouth shut and let nature run its course. You have no reason to mistrust Vera, and you know it. Honestly, Freddie, when did you become such a flat tire?"

The insult set the vein in Frederick's temple throbbing, but he let it pass. "It's just like you said, Rosie, I'm besotted. I can't think about anything else but her. This is it. She's the one."

Rosemary had never wanted to pummel her brother more than she did at that moment. "I could have told you that a long time ago. Vera, too, but neither of you ever listen to me. Perhaps if you did, you wouldn't be in this predicament."

"All right, all right. I get it. You're the smartest person alive and I'm an imbecile. Is that what you need to hear?" Frederick asked sarcastically.

"Yes, thank you," she replied happily. "Now, you need to fix this thing with Vera and move on. Life is too short to carry around a grudge, particularly since you have no reason to do so."

"I already said you were right, you don't need to rub it in," Frederick sulked.

Rosemary softened, for her brother had never cared enough for any other woman to experience the depth of feeling he struggled with now, and she really was thrilled to see that Vera was the one to turn him into a puddle of emotions.

"I'm sorry, truly. I'm out of sorts myself."

Frederick sat down across from her and peered at his sister. "I can see that. What's twisting up your knickers?"

"Charming, Freddie," she said with a roll of her eyes. "It's this house. I feel like the walls are beginning to close in on me."

"In this place? Try living in Pardington, with Mother and Father watching your every move. To hear Mother talk, you'd think I'm a absolute wastrel. But I suspect," he said, noting the pained expression on her face, "that you meant something quite different."

Rosemary sipped her tea slowly in an effort to delay the

inevitable conversation. "I'm rolling around in here, surrounded by staff I don't really need."

Frederick looked around, as if expecting Wadsworth to pop out of the woodwork.

"He's not here, none of them are. I gave them all the day off." That garnered an eyebrow raise from Frederick, but he kept quiet and let her continue. "It was one thing when Andrew was alive, and we planned on having children to fill the place up, but with him gone, well, it seems frivolous and unnecessary."

"Rosie, dear, you'll still fill this place with children. Not Andrew's, but perhaps Max's."

"I've thought about that, of course, but it feels...wrong somehow, to expect Max—or anyone else, for that matter—to live here in Andrew's shadow. I think that's part of why Vera doesn't want to move in. I think it makes her uncomfortable."

He ran his hands through his blond ringlets and said, "Don't you know your friend at all? She's not dragging her feet because she can't stand to live here. I believe I might have something to do with that, though she hasn't said as much. What she has expressed is that she feels if she moves in, you'll be inclined to stay here as well. She knows you better than you know yourself. Vera has a knack for seeing into a person. I believe she anticipated you'd feel the way you do now."

Rosemary's heart fluttered, and her eyes threatened to well with tears. "Yes, I suppose she would have, wouldn't she? I'm lucky to have her in my life. We both are. You, my dear brother, need to go buy the biggest diamond on display at Parsons, and make sure she doesn't get away!"

Frederick grimaced. "I'm not positive even the biggest

diamond at Parsons would get her to forgive me. I was a real cad, wasn't I?"

"I'll refrain from answering that question," Rosemary replied with a wink. "Rubbing salt in your wounds isn't as fun when you're being nice."

"Somehow, that's just as painful."

Rosemary mused over the conversation with her brother for a solid hour, until Vera tripped back into the house with a spring in her step. She stopped short at the sight of Frederick, and the tension was palpable. Beating a hasty retreat seemed prudent, but also dangerous, and so Rosemary remained seated and merely watched the drama unfold.

"Frederick, what are you still doing here?" Vera demanded, her jovial mood deflated.

"My car arrives in an hour, and I'll be out of your way," he replied. "If that's what you really want."

Vera's nostrils flared. "What I really want is your approval, not your suspicion."

"Of course you have my approval. Don't I go to rehearsals and opening nights and don't I hobnob with your theater friends?"

"Acting is my passion," Vera's voice went dangerously quiet. "It's a part of my life I won't give it up for anyone, not even you."

Even to Rosemary, Vera's words sounded like an ultimatum, while in all fairness, Frederick hadn't asked for any such thing.

He must have felt the same because his face reddened, and he spat out, "I could see quite clearly your *passion* for your work. The entire theater can see it three times a week! I'll throttle that Rod Stone if I have to see him put his lips on you again!"

"You mean Floyd Wilkins? That's his real name, Fred. He's not some Lothario. So far from it, in fact, that you appear even more ridiculous than you understand. He's. Not. Interested in me. Nor I in him."

Frederick balked. "You can't possibly know that. I saw him up there, and he appeared to be enjoying himself."

"That's pure theater," Vera retorted wryly. "It's what he's being paid to do, and evidently he's done a mighty fine job if even you can't see the truth. Furthermore, he's been nothing but polite to you. You're acting a fool, and I can't stand it!"

With that, Vera burst into tears and raced up the stairs. Frederick started after her, stopped short, shook his head, and then set out again before having third thoughts and sinking miserably into a seat near his sister.

"Don't. Just don't say anything," he warned. "I'll be on the next train out of the city. It's what's best for everyone. Perhaps this was a mistake after all."

He looked as though he might burst into tears himself, and as desperately as Rosemary wanted to say something that would cheer him, she knew it was best to keep her mouth shut.

Instead, she gathered herself and went to him for a moment, laid a hand on his shoulder gone wooden with tension and misery. When he didn't lean in for comfort, but rather turned and walked away, her heart broke for him.

TWENTY-THREE

The next morning, after a long day—and an even longer evening—consoling Vera, Rosemary woke feeling nearly as exhausted as she'd been when she went to sleep. She'd snuggled back beneath the covers, and was on her way to dreamland when Anna knocked softly on the door.

"What is it, Anna?" she asked sleepily.

"I'm sorry to wake you, but Wadsworth sent me up to tell you Mrs. Whittington has rung and asked for you. She said the nurse didn't arrive today and could you call on her at your earliest convenience?"

Rosemary sighed and sat up, wiping the sleep out of her eyes and saying a silent goodbye to the fleeting image of her dream.

"I'll get dressed and call on her right away."

She wondered, while she readied herself, why Ariadne hadn't simply called the service for another nurse and then remembered the way she'd treated the first one. If Max thought he was going to be able to force her to rely on paid staff, he must be mad, she decided.

Arriving at the cottage, Rosemary found Ariadne in a tizzy.

"The doctor has been in and out all day. Nurses coming and going, and Cliff has been out at least twice, returning with bags from the chemist. I tell you, that woman is in danger. I don't doubt the next car to arrive will be the coroner's van!"

"Ariadne," Rosemary said, treading lightly. "Please, sit down. Now, explain to me what happened with your nurse before we discuss the situation next door." The last thing she wanted to do was to lose favor with Max's mother, but she couldn't ignore Ariadne's growing obsession with her neighbors. One that Rosemary thought had merit, but still needed proving.

"I don't know," Ariadne snapped, refusing the proffered seat. "She simply didn't arrive here when she was supposed to." Her eyes didn't quite meet Rosemary's, and her cheeks turned a delicate shade of pink.

Rosemary raised an eyebrow but said nothing.

Finally, after a few moments of silence, Ariadne admitted, "If you must know, I told her not to come. This one is worse than the first one. She forces me to sit all day long, never giving me a moment to stretch my legs, and has flat out refused to allow me into the gardens. I feel like a prisoner in my own home!"

As much as she wanted to reprimand Ariadne for stretching the truth, Rosemary could understand the frustration she was feeling. Having been staunchly independent for most of her life, it must seem like the worst kind of insult to be managed by one's own offspring.

"Max will be angry, you know," she said gently.

Ariadne nodded once. "I do. I'll handle my son, but I need your help with Dolly."

"What is it you think I should do? He's never going to let me inside, and even if he did, how would I be able to help her?

If Cliff wanted Dolly dead, why would he have a doctor in attendance?"

"I want you to smell her tea," Ariadne said, matter-of-factly. "Poison hemlock has a musty smell that resembles urine."

Rosemary's nose wrinkled at the thought. "Oh, well, that sounds lovely. I'll just march on over and ask if I might take a sniff."

With a wave of her hand, Ariadne brushed aside Rosemary's sarcastic comment. "If we have proof, my son will have to listen, and then he can intervene."

More than anything, Rosemary wanted to refuse, but arguing with Ariadne had proved futile in the past, and she expected this time to be no different.

Between Max's need for irrefutable proof and his mother's disregard for procedure, Rosemary felt as if there was no space for inactivity. Perhaps, if she were able to find some solid evidence for or against Cliff, the situation could be resolved.

With nurses going in and out, she might be able to slip inside, assuming he left the house again. Weighing her options, she decided she'd risk Cliff's wrath if it meant gaining Ariadne's approval.

"All right, but you have to promise that if I come back empty handed, you'll stay out of Cliff's business from now on."

Ariadne agreed, and the pair set up a signal while they watched and waited for the man to leave the house. An hour later, still waiting, Rosemary began to get impatient. "If he's already been out twice, he's probably not going to leave again. I have an idea."

She marched into the other room and picked up the telephone.

When Cliff came on the line, she channeled Vera's acting skills and used a—rather convincing—fake voice. "Mr. Joseph, this is Lindy from the chemist shop. It seems you forgot to take one of your packages. Would you like to come back and pick it up?"

Cliff huffed and puffed, and rudely insinuated that if he'd left something there, it was the chemist's fault, but agreed to come by shortly.

"There," Rosemary said. "Now we've got an opening." A few moments later, Cliff exited the front door in a huff, slamming the garden gate behind him, leaving her the perfect opportunity to strike.

TWENTY-FOUR

Rosemary crept to the edge of the hedgerow bordering Ariadne's and the Josephs' gardens, looked around surreptitiously, and darted onto the verandah. She could hear some movement from inside and, quite stealthily, flattened herself against the front of the house and peeked through the window of the front door.

To the left of the entrance hall was a sitting room that spanned the edge of the house that looked onto the gardens. Through that, she could see an open doorway and a dining room, and guessed that the kitchen was located somewhere near the back. To the right of the hall, she spotted a set of stairs leading up to the second floor bedrooms, and when a maid came bustling down, she guessed that's where Dolly was busy convalescing.

Rosemary waited for the door at the end of the corridor to swing shut and then, quick as a cat, she opened the front door and tiptoed up the stairs. Blood pumped in her ears, and she pushed away the thought of what might happen should Cliff come home and find her there.

Every door on the upper floor was closed, which left Rosemary no choice but to search for Dolly behind each of them. The first one she tried turned out to be a closet, and the second a seldom-used guest bedroom judging by the slightly musty scent of infrequently laundered linens.

Behind the third, which looked out towards the gardens running between the house and Ariadne's, she found Dolly amid a pile of feather pillows, a tray of tea untouched by her side.

When she entered, the woman looked up as if in a daze.

"Who's there?" she asked, her voice barely above a whisper. Her forehead gleamed with sweat, yet she shivered beneath a pile of blankets.

"It's Rosemary Lillywhite, Ariadne Whittington's friend," Rosemary explained, closing the door quietly behind her and settling into the chair at Dolly's bedside. She tried to ignore how sickly Dolly appeared, but her own face turned white as a sheet at the sight of her.

Dolly squinted, stared for almost a full minute and finally said, "Rosemary...oh yes, I remember you." Rosemary wasn't convinced she did. She took a the opportunity to lean over and catch a whiff of the tea, and though it did have a pungent scent that wasn't particularly pleasant, it didn't resemble the urine that Ariadne had described. She let out a sigh of relief, and prepared to make a quick getaway when Dolly began to mumble.

"I'm dying, you know," she said, though her unfocused gaze didn't reach Rosemary's.

Rosemary's stomach did a little flip, and she covered one of Dolly's chilled hands with her own. She didn't know what to say, and realized it mattered little.

"Don't say that, Delores," Rosemary said gently, and the woman stirred.

"No, no," Dolly said. "Delores...she left. Gone...far..away..."

Rosemary couldn't fathom what she was talking about, but before she had time to ask any more questions, the sound of one of the nurses ascending the stairs interrupted Dolly's rambling.

Rosemary looked frantically around for a place to hide. She rose, and quickly ducked into a door she hoped was a closet opposite the bed. She shut the door, peeked through the keyhole, and let out a breath.

While the maid replaced the tea tray and fussed about tending to Dolly, a loud keening sound pierced the air and Rosemary's heart dropped into her stomach.

It was Ariadne's bird whistle, and it meant that Cliff had returned. She didn't know what he might do to her if he found her in his wife's bedroom, but she doubted he would be pleased. At the very least, Max would have to come and arrest her for trespassing, and the last thing she wanted to hear was another of his diatribes regarding her behavior.

She let out a sigh of relief when the maid finished her work, exited, and made her way down the stairs. Now, though, Rosemary was stuck, because she could hear Cliff's baritone voice carrying from below. Another search of the room left her with one possible exit: the window, outside which, if she remembered correctly, was a trellis she hoped would be sturdy enough to support her weight.

Throwing caution—and all sense of propriety—to the wind, she dashed from her precarious sanctuary, threw up the sash, and stuck one leg out the window. Dolly stirred again and tried to turn her head in Rosemary's direction, then squinted against the sunlight pouring through the curtains and finally closed her eyes. Rosemary climbed down far enough to still reach the window sash, returning it to its original position just in time to hear Cliff step into the room.

She continued her descent quietly, and landed on the grass with a thump. Her heart raced, and she looked up to the window and let out a relieved breath when she saw that the curtains still hung closed.

Next door, she could see Ariadne on the verandah, and for a moment thought she might have got away scot free. That is, until Duke caught sight of her and let out a yip of excitement. He ran right up to the fence, nimbly sidestepping Ariadne's attempts to corral him, and began a song and dance that was certain to attract the attention of anyone who happened to be within earshot: including Cliff, who would need only to peek out through the upstairs window to find Rosemary skulking around in his garden.

Making a beeline for the potting shed, Rosemary ducked inside and after a couple more dejected barks, Duke finally quieted down. She leaned her back against the door to catch her breath, and looked up to take in the scene before her.

Twenty-Five

Deep shelves lined one wall, each filled with jars of dried herbs, flowers, and seeds, and another, shorter wall held an assortment of gardening tools. More herbs hung from a complicated web of string that spanned from wall to wall, their delicate scents blending together to hang in a cloud around Rosemary's head. While meticulously organized, nothing about any of those things seemed out of the ordinary to be found in a potting shed.

What did, however, seem quite out of the ordinary was the chemist's lab laid out on the table in the center of the room. It was the one place where order seemed less of a concern. Beakers and flasks filled with liquids of varying viscosities connected to each other via a series of tubes that made Rosemary think of Mary Shelley's classic tale.

She took a step closer to examine the beakers situated around the makeshift lab, and one in particular caught her eye. It was a small vial filled with a silvery liquid, and she immediately recognized it as mercury—the same type used in thermometers just like the ones Cliff had purchased from the hardware store two days before.

A memory flashed through her mind and she could hear the voice of Mr. Chauncy, who taught science in her fourth year.

He'd warned the class about the dangers of coming into contact with a broken mercury thermometer.

Someone Mr. Chauncy had known—Rosemary couldn't remember who now, perhaps a sister or a cousin—had been poisoned by the stuff and died. When he'd described the symptoms, one of the boys in her class decided to poke fun, shaking and convulsing in an imitation of the tremors Mr. Chauncy described. The boy had been delivered a rather harsh punishment for his efforts, and as a result every time Rosemary heard the word thermometer, she pictured the scene.

She remembered the way Dolly's hands shook when she picked up her teacup, and a chill ran up her spine. Ariadne had been right about Cliff, though the poison he was using wasn't hemlock; it was mercury. She didn't dare touch the vial, but was reluctant to leave without some sort of proof of Cliff's treachery. Her eyes lit upon the rubbish bin sitting in the corner between a bank of shelves and a wall of gardening tools.

Rosemary bit her lip and made a snap decision. She donned a pair of gloves she found hanging from a nail on the wall beside her and reached into the half-full bin, pushing aside the detritus until a torn bit of parcel paper printed with the name Bernardes Trading caught her eye.

The scrap was wedged into the corner of the bin, and she had to practically climb inside in order to reach it. Just as her fingers met the paper, she heard Ariadne's bird whistle again. If the call had been a real one, the bird in question would have been in some sort of mortal peril, as it trilled, frantically, several times in a row.

Simultaneously, Duke erupted into a fit of growling barks, and Rosemary knew those two things occurring at the same time could only mean that Cliff was coming. Not only was Cliff coming, but she was about to be trapped with him inside a potting shed full of dangerous chemicals and deadly weapons.

The door creaked open slowly to reveal his silhouette lit from behind by the sun. He closed the door, slowly, keeping his eyes on Rosemary the whole time. She shrunk back against the rubbish bin, her heart thundering.

He took a step forward, his eyes flicking to the paper bag still clutched in her hands, and said calmly, "What do you think you're doing in here?"

"I—I—" Rosemary stammered. "I was just—hoping to borrow a set of hedge clippers. Ariadne's misplaced hers and I wanted to—" she trailed off as Cliff's eyebrows reached for his hairline and it became clear he wasn't buying her story. "I'm sorry, I'll just go." Rosemary took a step towards the door but Cliff stepped in front of her, blocking the way.

"You're a snoop, just like that meddling woman. I can't have you going back and telling Inspector Whittington what you've seen here, can I? Yes, I know he's not in finance, and I know you've been spying on me. What did you hope to find?"

"N-nothing," Rosemary said, her eyes scanning the shed for an escape route and finding none. Duke had stopped barking, and suddenly, the only sound she could hear was the chirping of actual birds.

Her only hope was that Ariadne had been able to track Max down, and he was on his way. She just had to stall Cliff long enough for him to arrive or for her to make a break for it. She made an effort to keep her gaze on him and away from the laboratory table, but the vague notion of throwing something caustic in his face crossed her mind.

"Actually," Rosemary said, trying to buy herself some time, "I know all about the poison, and so does Mrs. Whittington. Getting rid of me won't help you, so you might as well let me go."

"I can't," Cliff said, "and you know it. You know too much. You should have stayed out of things that were none of our concern."

"I do know," Rosemary admitted, trying another tactic. "I know you want to kill that poor woman. She's your wife. Dolly is your wife and she loves you. How could you do this to her?"

Cliff's pupils dilated, and a faraway look crossed his face. "No!" he shook his head as if trying to dislodge a disturbing image. "Dolly will never be her..." his eyes cleared, and now he glared at Rosemary with more hate than before.

What is he babbling about? Rosemary thought to herself. She thought back to Dolly's ramblings. *She's gone...far away...* and suddenly some of the pieces began to fall into place. The neighbor's statement that Cliff's wife was a dancer despite the fact that Vera claimed she wasn't one. Dolly's seeming confusion over how long she and Cliff had been married. There was only one thing to do now, and she hoped it would work.

"Who is Delores?" Rosemary asked, trying to keep him calm in spite of the fact that her own heart was beating out of her chest.

"Delores is my wife!" he yelled, becoming even more agitated and pacing about the small enclosure. "Or she was, before she tried to leave me for another man! Now she's dead."

All the fight seemed to drain out of him, but Rosemary knew she shouldn't push her luck. Her only chance of getting out of the potting shed alive was to keep him talking until Max arrived.

"You killed her, too, didn't you?" Rosemary breathed.

Cliff's hands tightened into fists. "You already know the answer to that question. Delores said she wanted to discuss it," he resumed pacing while he talked, seemed to relish the process of unloading all the secrets he'd kept for so long. "She came back to the house, said she wanted to talk. I thought she wanted to reconcile, but all she wanted was to convince me to agree to a divorce. I couldn't do that, so I went into the kitchen under the guise of fixing a pot of tea and that's when I remembered the hemlock. She didn't even flinch when I offered her the cup, and I smiled while she drank it down."

"But then you found Dolly," Rosemary nudged.

"Yes," Cliff spat. "Then I found Dolly. She understood why I couldn't marry her legitimately. My sob story about an unfaithful wife leaving me for another man and another life tore at her heart strings. It was her who came up with the idea to pretend to be Delores. Her desire to be with me was all-consuming, for a time. I thought it would be different with her, but she's just like every other woman. I see the way she looks at other men, and I won't be fooled a second time!"

Rosemary highly doubted that Dolly had tried to step out on Cliff, but he'd become so twisted it didn't matter. The poor woman had been doomed from the beginning. Ariadne's comments regarding that notion had been justified all along. If only she hadn't been so concerned about placating Max, she might have been able to avoid becoming trapped in a potting shed with a deranged killer.

"You realize I can't let you walk out of here, don't you?" Cliff said, picking the hedge clippers off the wall and leering.

Suddenly, Rosemary wished she hadn't tried to use borrowing them as an excuse for being inside the potting shed. "Bloody isn't really my style, but I think I'll make an exception."

"People know I'm here. Ariadne knows. She's probably already called Max. You'll never get away with this!"

"Actually," Cliff said with an evil smile. "I called the good inspector when I saw you duck in here. He's halfway to Cambridge right now, tending to an urgent police matter. By the time he gets back, there won't be anything left of you for him to find. You see," he motioned towards the chemistry lab, "I've concocted a solution that will break down all the body's organs, tissues, and even bone at a highly accelerated rate."

Cliff looked at his equipment with an expression of adoration and devotion. He delved into a technical explanation, talking mostly to himself, and while he waxed on, Rosemary noticed a shadow moving across the wall behind him. Someone was making their way along the side of the shed, what looked like a weapon of some sort raised above its head, and she felt a glimmer of hope.

Then she saw, beneath the raised slats of the potting shed door, the toe of Ariadne's brown leather sandal, and her heart sank again. She'd hoped it would be Max come to her rescue, and even more concerning was the fact that when Cliff noticed she was there, it would only take one minor blow to incapacitate Ariadne.

Almost in slow motion, she saw Cliff notice the direction of her gaze, and turn his head ever so slightly in that direction. On pure impulse and powered by adrenaline, she seized a hoe from its hook on the wall to her right and whipped it across the chemistry lab, showering Cliff with shards of his most prized possession.

Simultaneously, Ariadne brought the weapon, which turned out to be a croquet mallet, down on the back of Cliff's head. His eyes widened and then rolled back, and he fell to his knees, slumped forward, and landed face down on the dirt floor. Ariadne let out a whoop of excitement, nearly jumping into the air much to Rosemary's surprise, and then bopped him on the head once more, just for good measure.

Twenty-Six

It seemed like mere moments before a constable arrived to take control of Cliff, and he was just dragging the semi-conscious man away when Max pulled up in front of the house. He goggled at the scene before him and then raced towards the cottage.

"What on earth has happened here?" he demanded, his eyes flicking between his mother and Rosemary.

"You should have seen us, Max! We took him down, didn't we, Rosemary?" Ariadne exclaimed, her eyes shining with excitement. Rosemary couldn't hold back a grin, despite the grim circumstances of the afternoon. "You saved my life, is what happened, but your actions were reckless."

"Oh, pish posh," Ariadne brushed aside her concern. "What was I supposed to do? Let him kill you and then come after me? What if he'd hurt Duke? He'll be hanged, you know. Turns out, he killed his first wife, and had Dolly pretend to be her."

"What?" Max asked, his gaze landing on Rosemary for a more coherent explanation.

"She's right. She's been right all along. Cliff *was* trying to poison Dolly, but not with hemlock. That's what he used to poison his first wife—or I suppose, his real wife." Her response wasn't any more illuminating than Ariadne's had been, which she realized by the way Max's right eyebrow shot into his hairline.

"Cliff was married to a woman named Delores. She tried to leave him, so he killed her with the poison hemlock. Then, he met Dolly, and sold her a story. He said his wife had been unfaithful and then run off with the man she'd been seeing. Dolly believed he wasn't able to get a divorce and took pity on him. She agreed to pretend to be Delores, which must have been quite easy since their names are similar and the original Mrs. Joseph wasn't terribly social anyway. It doesn't seem like anyone noticed the difference between the two women."

Max absorbed the information, but then shook his head. "Why was he trying to kill Dolly then?"

"Well, Cliff let his past haunt him, is what I think. He got it in his head Dolly was trying to do the same thing Delores did. I don't believe for one second she was stepping out, but Cliff did. So he poisoned her, this time with mercury."

"Why *do* you think he changed up the poison?" Ariadne asked. "That's the one thing I don't understand."

Rosemary jerked a thumb in the direction of Dolly's bedroom window. "What better way to both get rid of them both? Dolly is an orphan, so there isn't anyone to miss her, and if he'd succeeded, Cliff would have had Delores' death certificate, making him a free man. Someone needs to tell her family, if she had any, that she's dead. You'll take care of that, won't you, Max?"

"Of course," he answered, "but what about the body? Where *is* Delores Joseph?"

Rosemary's gaze shifted to Ariadne, and they exchanged a

look before saying in unison, "Buried underneath the hemlock."

"Duke has been trying to dig her up."

"Oh, for heaven's sake," Max said, shaking his head with rueful irritation as he realized just how spot on his mother had been in her estimation of Cliff Joseph. "I'll take care of all of it. For now, Rose, I'm taking you home. Mother, I want you to go lie down until I return, and I don't want to hear any argument or else I'll call that service and arrange for another nurse."

Ariadne agreed, but the expression on her face suggested she was merely placating her son. "Rosemary, I expect you for tea once things settle. And Max, my dear, you'd be right not to let this one get away."

TWENTY-SEVEN

"Inspector Whittington is here to see you," Wadsworth informed Rosemary, who for once was enjoying being looked after. Anna had tucked her into bed, she was surrounded by more books than she could read in a month, and every couple of hours, the cook sent something delectable to her room on a tea tray.

"Shall I let him in?"

"Of course, just give me a moment to collect myself and I'll be right down."

The butler raised an eyebrow. "While that's all quite proper, do you think you ought to be getting out of bed?"

"I'm perfectly all right, I wasn't hurt," Rosemary promised.

"Just shaken is all." She shooed him out of the bedroom, dressed, and met Max in the dining room a short time later.

He appeared just as, if not more, concerned about her than Wadsworth did.

"I'm sorry to have arrived unannounced," Max apologized, "but I've had an interesting call from Miss Dawson at the Mariott Gallery, and I thought you would want to know. It seems she's found another Renoir hidden in the studio."

Eyes widening in surprise, Rosemary's voice filled with skepticism. "Another Renoir?"

"Yes, and that's exactly why I stopped by. It seems the plot has thickened."

With renewed energy, Rosemary rose from her seat. "Well, let's go, then. This I have to see."

Wadsworth cleared his throat and when Max turned, he saw the butler glaring at him. If looks could kill, Max would have been six feet under.

"Are you certain you're up for it?" he asked Rosemary, ignoring Wadsworth entirely.

She waved away his concerns. "I'm perfectly fine. I wasn't hurt. I'm more worried about your mother. She was running on pure nerve when she went after Cliff, and I was worried once it wore off she'd discover she'd been injured."

"She's in perfect health. Declared her knee completely healed, and sent the nurse packing. Fair warning, however, she's over the moon about everything that happened. You're her new hero, and she has a fair number of expectations about our future, which we won't discuss at present," Max said, shushing any reply Rosemary may have been preparing. "Mother will be telling this story until her dying day, I can assure you."

"I suspect that's true," Rosemary mused. "Now, let's go see what's going on at the gallery. Perhaps we can remove that case from your docket as well." She gathered her things and sailed out the front door.

When they arrived, Sadie was already at the door. She pulled it open for them, and then closed and locked it behind her. "Aurora is on her way down, but she has a key. I'm not taking any more chances after what happened the other night," she explained.

She led them up the stairs to the studio, where a beautiful

work of art leaned against a table. Set against a background of dappled sunlight and trees, and depicted from behind, the figure of a young man faced a woman leaning on a swing. It was, as Renoir tended to paint, a scene of joy and happiness.

"I can't imagine why Sidney would hide this in here." The musing came from Sadie, who stood behind Rosemary while she crouched down to examine the piece.

"Because it's not real," Rosemary replied, standing up and dusting off her hands. "It's a forgery, and a rather spectacular one at that."

"A forgery?" Aurora's high-pitched exclamation pierced the air and startled the rest of the group, who had been so focused on the painting they hadn't noticed her arrival. "What on earth are you talking about? And what is *she* doing here?" Aurora pointed to Rosemary accusingly.

Max blanched, and though his response almost brought a grin to Rosemary's face, she did feel sorry for him. Having to deal with a woman like Aurora during the course of an investigation was one thing; that woman being a former paramour made his job all the more difficult.

"Miss Dawson called me, as she ought to have done, and I needed someone I trust, who also knows art, to consult. Do you have a problem with that?" he demanded, his voice icy.

Since there was no reasonable argument, Aurora acquiesced.

"No, of course not. I apologize." It wasn't sincere, but it mattered little. "How can you be positive it's a forgery?" she wanted to know. "This painting is called "The Swing," and it was shown at the third Impressionist Exhibitions in 1877 and immediately sold to a private collector. It has not, I assure you, come onto the market since, so there is no possibility that this is the original painting."

Rosemary turned abruptly and walked out of the studio, down the stairs and back into the gallery. Max followed her, trailed by Aurora and Sadie.

She approached the Renoir on display, and what she saw made her heart drop into her shoes. "They're both fakes." She turned to Aurora and pierced her with a stare. "Are these Sidney's work? He mentioned he dabbled, and you said he was a gifted painter."

"I—I—," Aurora stuttered. "I don't know," she finally finished, miserably.

"Where did Mr. Mariott say he acquired this piece?" Max demanded as if she hadn't spoken at all.

Her eyes shifted away from Max's piercing stare, and she mumbled again, "I don't know. I wasn't involved with the deal."

"I don't believe you," Max said harshly. "Mr. Mariott painted these forgeries and tried to pass at least one of them off as the real thing. Isn't that true?"

"You have no proof of that!" Aurora snapped. "And while you're here, examining paintings and making suppositions, Sidney is out there somewhere, possibly hurt or maybe even dead! "

Max hushed her and said, "There's nothing to indicate that's the case, and Mr. Matthews confirmed that Mr. Mariott left here of his own volition. From where I'm standing, it appears that Mr. Mariott got in over his head, took the money, and left town. You need to come to terms with the idea that he is not the man you thought he was. Unless, of course, you're involved."

The suggestion blew Aurora's wind up again, and she began to protest. "Why would I have called you in if I knew anything about these—those—any of this?"

"You're prepared to marry this man, Aurora. You say you know him better than anyone, and you've a stake in the success of this gallery. Yet, you don't know anything about where Mr. Mariott acquired the Renoir. Do you see how that might be difficult for me to believe?"

Aurora pressed her mouth into a thin line but didn't say anything.

"Silence won't help you, if you were involved," Max said harshly. "Furthermore, your name is on a significant portion of the paperwork. If Mr. Mariott doesn't return, you'll be the one to take the fall. Is that a sacrifice you're willing to make?"

"I'm telling you, I don't know!" Aurora cried. "Sidney is a good man, but he's a man. He makes the decisions. All I did was sign the lease. I've nothing to do with the artists or the pieces! You can't pin this on me, you've no proof," she wailed miserably.

Max clasped his hands together and said, "If that's the story you want to go with, be my guest. For now, we're at another standstill, which gives me plenty of time to dig deeper into Mr. Mariott's past—and yours, Aurora. If I find anything out of place, don't think our previous relationship will save you from being held responsible to the fullest extent of the law."

Sadie bit at her cuticle, though Rosemary doubted she had any skin left. Her fingers were red and her nails jagged. She looked as though she was going through some kind of internal struggle, and Rosemary flashed back to the previous afternoon when she'd been trapped in the potting shed with Cliff. His fingernails had also been bitten to the quick, and it hadn't taken much for him to crack and spill his story.

"Sadie," Rosemary said, her tone sharp, "if you know something, now is the time to come clean."

The girl stared at her for a moment and finally seemed to make up her mind. "All right," she said, sounding resigned. "I can't let Aurora take the blame for something I know she didn't do. You were right before, this wasn't a case of a robbery gone bad. In fact, there was no robbery at all."

The statement earned Sadie a matching set of incredulous stares. "What do you mean?" Max asked a moment later, having regained his composure first.

"I can't keep up this charade any longer," she said, sinking onto the stool that stood behind the reception counter. "Sidney staged the robbery the night after the opening. Before you ask, I don't know why. I came in through the back door that evening. I'd just been evicted, and I needed a quiet place to collect my thoughts."

Sadie paused a moment, took a deep breath. "Sidney must have been in the studio, but the door was closed and I didn't see him anywhere. I went into the office and noticed the deposit bag and the cash laid out on the desk. I figured he must be around somewhere, and thought I'd just tidy up a bit before asking him if I could sleep on the couch in the office for the night. I'd just taken a stack of papers into the file closet when I heard some banging coming from the studio. I got scared, so I closed the closet door and turned off the light."

As the story progressed, Aurora pressed one hand over her heart as if scared to hear more. In a rush, Sadie got the rest out.

"It was Sidney and Fritz, the security guard he uses when we host an event. I thought it was odd he was here, but figured maybe he was looking for his payment. My heart stopped pounding and I was just about to reveal myself when I realized it wasn't money Fritz was there for; it was another job. Sidney said he had to hide the cash for a while, and that he'd have to disappear along with it if he was going to get 'that weasel' off his back. He asked if Fritz had a pocket knife and then I heard a grunt of pain. My guess is that Sidney didn't have the stomach to cut himself, and so Fritz did the dirty work."

Rosemary's eyes lit up. "It does explain the bandage Fritz was wearing when I saw him at the pub the night after Vera's play. But why didn't you say anything before?"

"That's what I'd like to know," Max agreed.

"Because, well, I'm in a bad place," Sadie explained. "It didn't sound like Sidney was planning on taking off for good, just disappearing for a bit. I figured if I kept quiet, I'd get paid enough to get back into my landlord's good graces. I can't keep sleeping at the gallery, or at Aurora's place. Besides, Sidney has always done right by me, and I thought I was protecting him."

Although Rosemary could understand the inclination, she knew Max was furious that Sadie had withheld information on an open investigation. Aurora, however, looked like she might spit nails at the girl.

"You could have told me what happened, Sadie. I've been frantic with worry," the woman said acerbically.

Sadie squared her shoulders and faced Aurora. "While I appreciate everything you've done for me and mean no disrespect, it was *you* who called in the police. I'd every intention of informing you about Sidney, but telling you about it after the inspector got involved would have made you an accessory. I thought if he came back, it would be a moot point, and all would be well. If you've got to arrest me, Inspector Whittington, I understand."

Max rubbed the bridge of his nose, his eyes closed as if deep in thought. When he opened them again he trained them on Aurora. "You—or Mr. Mariott, I suppose—have one of the most loyal employees I've ever seen. I suggest you pay her well enough so she can keep up on her rent going forward. This is rather an unusual case. Sidney is the owner of this business, so he had every right to take the money and do whatever he likes with it. No actual crime has taken place, and though we don't know where he is, Sidney isn't technically missing. Therefore, I'm going to let Miss Dawson's involvement go. What I won't let go is this business with the forgeries. People have been duped out of their money paying to see a fake painting."

"Sidney didn't know it wasn't a real Renoir. He even had it authenticated by an independent art expert. Let me show you."

Sadie led the troupe into the office, which had been cleaned up and reorganized, most likely by Sadie herself during the time she was sleeping at the gallery.

"Here, it says 'fee for art appraisal' and a name, Wentworth Price."

Max picked up the telephone and asked the operator for the number of a Wentworth Price. He listened for a moment, and then said, "You're certain, nowhere in London?" He asked a few more questions, his brow furrowing into a deeper indent all the while.

"All right, thank you."

He replaced the receiver and explained, "There's no Wentworth Price in London, and no art appraisers listed under any similar names. It's possible he's in the employ of another expert, but it will take some digging to get any more information. Sidney obviously met with someone, though, and I intend to get to the bottom of it. Whichever of you has pull with this Fritz fellow, call him and get him to come down here. Say whatever you need to say. I want this case wrapped up, and after that I never want to attend a gallery opening for the rest of my life."

Twenty-Eight

It took over an hour for Fritz to arrive at the gallery, during which time Aurora pushed Max into fine state. She wouldn't stop fretting over where Sidney was and what was going to happen to him when he returned. All attempts to discover who was the weasel he'd mentioned during the faked robbery were moot, since Aurora appeared to have very little knowledge of her fiancé's activities.

Rosemary avoided speaking with her, partly because she found the woman a trial to deal with, and also because she knew if she opened her mouth, something uncharitable might come out.

How Aurora could be so clueless was beyond Rosemary's ability and willingness to comprehend, and if the woman been anyone other than a former paramour of Max's, it might have been sympathy she felt instead of disdain.

"Where is Sidney?" Fritz asked after Aurora let him into the building. Max had retreated to the upstairs office in case Fritz decided to make a run for it at the sight of a detective inspector, but Rosemary watched from the landing.

Aurora locked the door behind him, tilted her nose in the air, and said, "Follow me."

When he entered the office, his eyes widened at the sight of

Sadie, Rosemary, and Max gathered there. "I thought you said Sidney was back."

"I lied," Aurora replied airily. "You should be familiar with the concept since you're the one who helped him disappear in the first place. I've been worried sick, and for nothing."

"I remember you. You were here the night of the opening," he said, his gaze focused on Max. "You're a cop, and I've got nothing to say to you. Don't know anything about where Sid went off to."

Max cleared his throat and fixed Fritz with a stare. "How do you know he *went off* to anywhere, then?"

"Well—well—," Fritz stuttered, "S'pose I don't know for certain." He eyed the door, taking a step back as he spoke.

"Don't bother trying to run," Max warned. "There's no need for you to lie, either. We know Mr. Mariott wasn't in any danger that night and that you were helping him. All I want is answers, I'm not looking to lock you up. Cooperate, and I'll keep your name out of it."

That to his knowledge, Fritz hadn't actually committed a crime, Max did not reveal. His ploy worked, and Fritz nodded. He tried to fit his bulky frame into one of the chairs opposite the desk and, failing, took a seat on the sofa instead.

"What do ya wanna know?"

"Why don't you start with why you assisted Mr. Mariott in staging a crime scene at his own gallery."

Fritz cracked his knuckles loudly and then said, "Sid called, so I came. Said he was in some kinda trouble, needed help getting out of a scrape. Said he'd lay low for a bit and that he'd pay me a bonus when he got back. S'all I know."

"I certainly hope that's not the case," Max replied with a

raised eyebrow. "In fact, I know it isn't. I understand you were present when Mr. Mariott met with an expert art appraiser—the man who authenticated the Renoir hanging in the gallery. What can you tell me about that?"

"Not much, I s'pose. Thought it was odd he wanted me to be there—probably thought this guy might try to lift the thing, but the meet went off without a hitch."

Max exchanged a look with Rosemary. "But you saw the appraiser. Can you describe him?"

Fritz's nose scrunched up and his eyes went unfocused, as though he were trying to remember. "Handsome chap, I'll give 'im that. Tall, dark hair."

Max sighed, frustrated. "This is a fool's errand. The man you're describing could be anyone."

"Hang on," Rosemary said. "Maybe we can do better. Hand me a piece of paper and a pencil, Sadie, please."

Sadie complied, and Rosemary set to sketching. She talked Fritz through the process, and when she was finished, she turned the paper around to show Max. "He looks familiar, doesn't he?" "That's the man from Vera's play. Her co-star. Rod Stone, correct?"

"It certainly is," Rosemary replied. "It seems to me that Sidney got hoodwinked. Except, we're missing something. Rod might be a gifted actor, but he doesn't possess the mental faculties to perpetrate a scheme as complicated as this one. Nor, do I believe, does he have any motive to do so."

"I suppose we'll have to pay him a little visit," Max said with a sigh. "I assume Vera knows where I can find him?"

TWENTY-NINE

od Stone—or rather Floyd Wilkins or Wentworth Price — wasn't hard to get hold of. He lived in a small flat around the corner from the theater, and Vera was more than happy to help Rosemary and Max with the interrogation.

"You know this is highly irregular," Max grumbled. "I should have brought you straight home and attended to this matter myself."

He mumbled something about losing his job, but Vera happily defended his choice to involve them. "You'll get more out of him with me here. He's an odd duck, and I doubt he'll talk to you on your own. Besides, Rosemary's been involved in loads of investigations by now, and it's always come out tops in the end. Don't the police consult with private detectives all the time?"

"Yes," Max said slowly, "but—"

Rosemary cut in, "What he's trying not to say is that they consult with *male* detectives."

"Well, perhaps it's time for a change," Vera replied as they pulled up in front of the block of flats where Rod lived.

The corridor was dark with no windows, illuminated only by a single hanging bulb, but the floors were free of debris and the scent of disinfectant almost covered the stench of curry that wafted up from the Indian restaurant below.

Three knocks on the door with no answer or movement from inside almost had Max deciding to give up, but finally after the fourth round of banging, Rod answered, his voice thickened with sleep.

"I'm coming," he said irritably. "Oh, hello, Vera." His eyes widened when Max stepped into view. "What can I do for you?"

"Let us in, for starters," she replied, sailing past him and inside without waiting for an invitation.

Rod simply stared at Vera with a dumbfounded expression and joined her where she'd settled onto his sofa.

"What's this all about?" he asked, his eyes shifting to Max, who had refrained from sitting down and was standing with his arms crossed, looking formidable. Rosemary was keen to allow the two of them to handle the situation, and focused on watching Rod's reactions rather than participating in the interrogation. It was Vera's turn this time, and she appeared delighted to complete the task. Rosemary almost felt a little sorry for Rod.

"We need to know how you're connected to Sidney Mariott," Vera said bluntly. "And don't bother trying to lie. You'll just make it more difficult on yourself."

"She's right," Max said, "talk, Mr. Wilkins. Or I'll make sure you're sorry you didn't."

Rod glanced towards the door, as if he might make a run for it after all, and then all but dissolved. "It was just a job. Freelance, you know. An audition, he said."

"Who said?" Vera demanded.

"Gregory was his name. Gregory Newcastle. He came to my last show—you know, that production in the park. I played a detective who kept missing the most obvious clues. It was a choice comedic gig, and I pulled it off brilliantly, if I do say so myself.

Anyway," he said, noting Max's narrow-eyed warning to get to the point. "Mr. Newcastle caught me after the show and asked if I'd like to join some sort of company he was putting together. He said all I needed to do was ace the audition, and I'd be in. He gave me some notes and a basic character sketch, but he said it was supposed to test my improvisational skills. He said I'd have to commit to the role and convince his associate that I was who I said I was."

Vera nodded in understanding, as if that type of thing was a common occurrence. Perhaps it was, Rosemary thought. It wasn't as though she were well-versed in the inner workings of the theater crowd.

"The character was an art expert, and I was given information about the painting I was supposed to pretend to authenticate," Rod explained. "I did the job, and then when Daisy invited me to the gallery opening, and I realized what I'd actually done. Mr. Mariott was furious with Mr. Newcastle. He said he'd get what was coming to him, but the guy just laughed and said there wasn't anything he could do without implicating himself in the process. I just wanted to get out of there, so I gave Daisy my best wishes and left. I have no idea what happened next. Am I being arrested?"

"Wait a second," Rosemary said before Max could answer. "We were all there that night, and I saw you and Sidney talking to—" Rosemary clapped her palm against her forehead as she remembered the scene that had played out before her eyes.

"Of course! I can't believe I didn't see it before. Those paintings—the forgeries—they were done by Reno Riley. I knew there was something familiar about the brush work, but he's so derivative, his own style got lost in a mishmash of other impressionist techniques. Aurora was right. It wasn't Sidney's fault."

"Does this mean I'm *not* being arrested?" Rod squeaked into the silence that followed Rosemary's pronouncement.

Max sighed, and shook his head. "No, but you're going to do whatever you can to help us find Mr. Riley and make sure he's held accountable for his crimes. For now, you're to stay here, and if he tries to contact you, call me." He pulled a card out of his pocket and handed it to Rod.

"Um...well, you see..." Rod hedged, his face white as a sheet. "I did receive a message from Mr. Newcastle—I mean Mr. Riley, asking me to call him if I was up for another job. I have no intention of returning his call. I want no part of his racket."

Rosemary had to purse her lips to keep from laughing at his expression and wished Frederick were there to see it. He'd never be intimidated by Floyd Wilkins again.

"Another job?" Rosemary said thoughtfully. "He's going after Arthur Banks now, I'm sure of it. Daisy said Mr. Banks had a line on another Renoir. It's too big a coincidence."

Max exchanged a look with Rosemary, one that indicated they were both thinking along the same line. "You're going to call him back," Max said to Rod, his tone brooking no refusal. "You're going to accept that job, and you're going to do exactly what I tell you to do. Do you understand?"

THIRTY

"Are you positive you're up for this, Mr. Banks?" Max asked the gallery owner after they'd laid the plan out. "We wouldn't want to put you in an awkward position."

With a dramatic wave of his ever-present pince-nez, Arthur Banks dismissed Max's concern. "Reno Riley has already perpetrated enough crimes against art with that display of his at the Mariott Gallery. I won't let him commit another one if there's anything I can do to stop him. Furthermore, I won't be taken for a fool." He tossed a wink in Rosemary's direction.

"Well, we appreciate your cooperation," Max replied. "Now, I believe all our ducks are in a row. It's nearly show time, so let's all get into position." He kissed Rosemary on the cheek and exited the building.

Rosemary walked around the space, taking in the collection Mr. Banks had put together. "They're all up-and-coming artists with considerable talent, at least in my opinion," he said, watching her intently. "Your friend Daisy would do well here."

Vera was busy checking her appearance in a mirrored compact she'd fished from the depths of her handbag and replied in between dabbing another coat of lipstick. "We'll be certain to mention your open-ended offer next time we see her. I'm certain she'll be appreciative, particularly since the future of

Mr. Mariott's establishment hasn't been decided as of yet. There," she declared, snapping the compact closed. "Do I look like I've got money to spend on expensive art?"

"You *do* have money to spend on expensive art," Rosemary said ruefully. "But you certainly look lovely. Now, let's find our marks and wait." The pair allowed Mr. Banks to show them to a concealed corridor near the rear exit of his gallery and settled in to wait for their cue.

"Did you thoroughly enjoy the expression on Aurora's face when Max told her she wouldn't be taking part in the caper? I thought she might scratch his eyes out," Vera said with a twinkle in her own.

The memory made Rosemary's lips turn up into a grin that bordered on evil. "I certainly did. With any luck, this will all be over soon, and I'll never have to see that woman again in my life."

Thoughts of an evening out with Max that didn't involve crime, subterfuge, and ex-sweethearts flitted through her mind, and she had to drag her attention back to the matter at hand. A few long minutes later, the gallery door opened and in strode Reno carrying a carefully wrapped package. Rod Stone followed after, looking quite snazzy in a suit and tie.

"Mr. Banks, good to see you," Reno said smoothly, leaning the package against the waiting empty easel Arthur had supplied and reaching out to shake the man's hand. "This is Wentworth Price, art expert," Reno introduced Rod without flinching. "He does all my authenticating, and I think you'll find he's top notch." Rosemary peeked around the corner and relished the thought that soon, they'd wipe that smug look right off Reno's face.

"Yes, well, we'll see about that," Arthur replied. "If you've got what you say you've got, we'll all walk out of here pleased. If you don't, well that's another story. My client is very discerning, you know."

"Your client?" Reno asked, his eyes narrowing to slits. "What client?"

Vera stepped out from her hiding place, Rosemary in tow, her heels clicking over the tile. "That would be me," Vera said smoothly, sashaying over to Reno and taking her seat next to Arthur without bothering with a more formal introduction.

"I hope you don't mind, but I've brought along my own expert." Vera gestured to Rosemary, who had to fight to keep a smirk from spreading across her face.

"No, no, of course not," Reno said, having recovered from the surprise. "The more the merrier. I simply thought you wanted the Renoir for display in the gallery. I presume it would look far better on the walls of a home befitting a glamorous woman such as yourself," he said smoothly, ogling Vera as though she were a juicy steak that had been set before him. "Didn't I meet you at the Mariott Gallery opening? You were with a rather overprotective man, as I recall."

Rosemary guessed it took a concerted effort for Vera to keep her cool, and not for the first time was she impressed with her friend's acting skills. "Oh, you know how men are. Why don't we dispense with the chit-chat and get down to business?"

Reno held his hands up in surrender and laughed. "Your wish is my command." He unwrapped the painting and placed it back on the easel, stepping back so everyone could admire it. "Here she is," he said dramatically. "It's one of Renoir's greatest works: *Dance at Le moulin de la Galette*."

As forgeries went, Reno's was stunning in the way he mimicked the master's color palette across the veritable sea of figures in the painting. The dappled sunlight flitting around the dancing figure on the left spoke of ability that Reno should have used for his own work rather than in the commission of a crime.

"As you can see," Rod began his rehearsed spiel, "this piece exemplifies Renoir's fluid brush strokes, and his treatment of light and shadow."

"Do you take us for fools?" Rosemary asked icily, feeling vindicated. "That painting is on display at the Luxembourg Museum in Paris. This is obviously a forgery."

Instead of backing down, Reno smiled languidly and said, "It seems you don't know your art history as well as you think you do. Pierre-Auguste Renoir painted two copies of this piece, and this is the smaller one."

Rosemary balked, pulled a magnifying glass out of the case she'd brought along, and approached the painting. After several moments, she drew back, shock coloring her features. "It's authentic," she declared, her voice deadpan.

"Of course it's authentic," Reno replied. "I wouldn't come here trying to sell you a fake, now would I?"

His hubris grated on her last nerve, and Rosemary snapped.

"It wouldn't be the first time, would it?" She let the statement sink in, and watched as Reno tried to recover.

"I don't know what you mean," he said smoothly, though his eyes darted around the room as if he were looking for an escape route should the need arise.

"I think you do," Rosemary retorted. "You paid this man," she said, gesturing to Rod, "to participate in your fraud, and you've bankrupted the Mariott Gallery in the process. How you came by this work of art, I've no idea, but I hardly believe it was through legitimate means."

Reno stood, and glared at Arthur. "I don't know what you're trying to pull, but it isn't going to work. I believe I'm no longer interested in selling this piece after all. Let's go, Mr. Price." He glanced at Rod, tilting his head towards the door.

"I think you'll find," Rod replied, "that escape will prove difficult."

There, outside the glass, stood Sidney Mariott, flanked by Aurora and Sadie. Sidney walked inside looking as though he might like to tear Reno's head off, and was making a visible effort to avoid doing so.

Rosemary exchanged a look with Vera. Sidney's presence wasn't only a surprise for Reno. "Where'd he come from?" Vera asked under her breath.

"I don't know," Rosemary whispered back, "but my guess is that Aurora and Sadie filled him in on our plan."

"Don't move," Sidney barked while Reno squirmed and made a rush at the painting.

That he thought he had any chance of getting away with the thing intact almost made Rosemary laugh out loud. "You're a dead man if you walk out that door," Sidney continued, pointing to where three figures stood leaning against a lamp-post across the street. "Got yourself in too deep, didn't you? Deep enough to stoop to selling off another forgery to another unwitting gallery owner."

"No! You don't understand," Reno held his hands up. "Listen, it's not a forgery. Not this time. It's the real deal, I swear."

"He's right," Rosemary said above the din. "It's real. What I'd like to know is, why sell Sidney the fake if you had an authentic piece all along?"

The vein in Reno's temple throbbed as he clenched his teeth and finally snapped, "It's a family heirloom, all right? My mother is one of the girls in this painting. I've spent my whole life recreating Renoir's work. I'd hoped the money I made off Sid here would get me out of my jam, but it didn't. They want more, and this is all I have left," he said miserably.

If he hadn't been such a cad, Rosemary might have felt sorry for him, but as it was, she couldn't muster up a morsel of sympathy. However, there were a few more questions that needed answering, and she wasn't prepared to allow Sidney to walk out the door before she learned the truth.

She spun on him and demanded, "Where have you been all this time? You've hurt Aurora, you've wasted Inspector Whittington's valuable time, and it appears as though you've no artists left to fill the walls of your gallery."

Taken aback, Sidney balked, "I don't know how that's any of your business."

"She's got a point, Sid," Aurora spoke up then. "I've been worried sick."

"I already told you I'm sorry, Aurora. Can't we discuss this later?"

Now it was Aurora's turn to balk. "Will you be here later, or will you have taken off again?" The pair dissolved into a domestic argument, shifting the tension away from Reno, who inched his way towards the painting.

"What was I supposed to do, Aurora?" Sidney continued, oblivious to Reno's attempts at escape. "Let him take all the money from the opening along with what I paid him for the Renoir? I was protecting us."

Behind the two bickering lovers, Reno's eyes scanned the back of the gallery for an alternate exit. When the argument reached its crescendo, he grabbed the Renoir and bolted towards the back door.

"Not so fast," Rod Stone stepped in front of him and rose to his full height, creating an impassable barrier the smaller man didn't have enough courage to challenge. "You're not going anywhere. Have you forgotten those men outside? You won't get far."

All the fight left Reno then, and his shoulders sank miserably. "I'm a dead man walking. They'll kill me if I don't bring them the money, or I'll go to prison and end up with a shiv in my belly."

Nervously, he gestured toward the three men across the street. "They're waiting for me now, and it isn't as though I hurt anyone. I'm not a violent man!"

"Do you think I care?" Sidney seethed. "You've all but bankrupted me already. I say you deserve whatever punishment you get."

Aurora gasped and stared at her fiancé, her face pale with horror. "You can't mean that, Sid," she cried. "And if you do, you're not the man I thought I was marrying." She met Rosemary's gaze, and appeared so miserable that Rosemary softened infinitesimally.

"There has to be another way where everyone gets what they're owed and what's deserved—but no more than that. I've got a proposition for you," she said, concocting a plan on the fly and making a snap decision she hoped she wouldn't regret. "I'll buy the Renoir from Reno, and I'll place it on loan to the Mariott Gallery until his debt has been paid."

Vera snorted and made a comment about not being the only one with money to spend.

Reno's eyebrows shot up, and she was treated to several gaping stares. Only Arthur Banks appeared dissatisfied with Rosemary's offer. "What about me?" he exclaimed. "I was offered that piece, I helped you with your little plot, and now I get nothing?"

"You'll get Daisy Kent out of the deal, and be happy for it," Rosemary retorted. "Now, what do you all say? I can call off the dogs, or I can sic them on you, Reno. It's your choice."

"I'm in. Whatever you want, just don't let them kill me."

Rosemary grinned, "Oh, you're in no danger of dying today." She went to the door and gestured to the three men who had Reno so scared.

Accompanied by Fritz and Wadsworth, Max strode in. "You remember Inspector Whittington, I presume? You'll want to go with him, Reno."

THIRTY-ONE

"Rosemary, are you up here?" Vera called from the landing leading to the attic. She heard a shuffling sound followed by a muffled voice coming from the bedroom that used to be Rosemary and Andrew's and stepped inside. "How's it coming?"

"I'm almost finished." Rosemary's voice quivered with emotion. "This is all that's left." She pointed to a framed painting depicting the banks of the Thames. It was the spot where Andrew had proposed and had hung in a place of honor above the mantle since they'd moved into the townhouse.

Vera peered at the piece and marveled at her friend's talent. "I wanted to talk with you, but perhaps this isn't the time."

"Nonsense," Rosemary replied, sounding stronger now. She sat down on the edge of the bed and bade Vera to join her. "What is it?"

"I can't move in with you, and I hope you don't hate me for saying that." Vera looked as though she might burst into tears, but Rosemary hushed her.

"I know," she said gently. "And I understand. Frederick and I had a long talk the other day and I realized I have a number of decisions to make. You moving in would only distract me from them, but I think you knew that already."

Vera dissolved then, and clung to her friend, spilling tears all over Rosemary's shoulder. "I pushed him away, didn't I?"

"Yes, you did," Rosemary admitted. "But he deserved some of what he got. Don't you fret about it. In fact, I've got something to cheer you up."

She led Vera down two flights of stairs and into the art studio that had been Andrew's office.

"But you were the one who was sad," Vera lamented the whole way. "I'm supposed to be cheering you up, not the other way around."

Rosemary duly ignored her.

"Here, I painted this for you. I got the idea in my head when we were at the gallery opening, and I've finally finished it." She pulled the protective sheet from the easel it covered, revealing a masterpiece that took Vera's breath away.

The canvas held a scene of a younger Rosemary and Vera walking hand in hand down a cobbled street, done in the impressionist style of Pierre-Auguste Renoir.

"It's like catching a glimpse of our former selves," Vera breathed. "Almost a memory come to life."

"That's exactly what I was aiming for," Rosemary said, wrapping an arm around Vera's shoulders. "When you and

Frederick get married, I expect it to be hung in a place of honor in your new home."

Vera's eyes welled again, and she shook her head. "I told you already, I've ruined it all."

"Not quite, you haven't," came Frederick's voice from behind them. He stood in the doorway, and when Vera whirled around to face him, he strode across the room and took her in his arms.

A mumble of apologies became muffled in their embrace, and when they broke apart Frederick got down on one knee.

"Vera Blackburn, I promise never to interfere with your work ever again. I promise to be the best man I can be, and to make you the happiest woman on earth. Will you be my wife?"

Vera never bothered to look at the ring nestled in black velvet that Frederick held up in offer. She couldn't have cared less what it looked like, but Rosemary took a peek and grinned. For once, her brother had listened and had bought the largest diamond Parsons had to offer.

***

Next time, it's murder for sure! Keep reading for a preview of Most Definitely Murder where you'll never guess whose good name Rosemary has to clear this time.
~Also Available in Audiobook & Paperback Editions~

QUICK AUTHOR'S NOTE

Hi, I'm Emily and I write intriguing mysteries wrapped in a layer of proper English snark. I live in Maine, USA with my boyfriend, cat, chocolate lab...and too many books to count. *And if you're not careful, I might just kill you off in one of my novels...*
But seriously, the inspiration for Rosemary Lillywhite came to me on a quiet afternoon while leafing through an old family photo album. Among the sepia-toned images was a photograph of a poised woman with an enigmatic smile, surrounded by an

air of timeless grace. She was a mystery herself—her story half-whispered in family lore and half-forgotten over generations. It made me wonder: what if a woman like her had secrets of her own, secrets she unraveled one thread at a time while solving mysteries?

From there, Rosemary began to take shape—smart, determined, and with an innate ability to see what others might overlook. She embodies the elegance of a bygone era and the tenacity of a modern sleuth, blending the best of both worlds.

Writing Rosemary has been a joy, and I hope you find her adventures as captivating as I do.

Thank you for joining her on this journey!

I'd love to offer you the chance to sign up for my newsletter—the best place to get new release updates, sales notifications, and other fun content.

Sign up, and as a thank-you gift for hanging out with me, you'll also get a FREE novella that isn't available anywhere else. And of course, I promise not to SPAM your inbox!

Love, hugs, and happy reading,

Emily Queen

P.S. If you enjoyed this book please consider leaving a review at your favorite store, Goodreads, or Bookbub. Your reviews help indie authors reach new readers!

Excerpt from Most Definitely Murder

Mrs. Lillywhite Investigates - Book 6

Rosemary Lillywhite searched the roadway for a black car, or more specifically, a black car manned by a rugged, six-foot-tall, sandy-haired man. Several of the ones parked along the side of the high street matched the description, but she couldn't find her butler, Wadsworth, among them.

"Well, he must have got caught up circling the block," she said with defeat to her dearest friend, Vera Blackburn. "Why don't we just walk and see if we come across him."

"It isn't as if we're laden with shopping bags," Vera grudgingly agreed. "The shops don't seem to have much in the way of tempting wares today." It was unlike Vera not to find at least one item to strike her fancy, and Rosemary sighed as the cloud that had been circling her friend's head all day grew darker still.

"Out with it," Rosemary demanded, beginning to stroll and pulling Vera along with her. "What on earth is bothering you?"

Vera hemmed and hawed for a few moments, her stride quickening, and finally threw her hands in the air. "My wedding is turning into a disaster! Our mothers have gone entirely insane. I fear by the time they're through, it will be the most ostentatious event of the century!"

"You must have known that when you decided to marry my brother, Mother was included in the deal," Rosemary reminded her. Evelyn Woolridge was a force of nature, certainly, and she'd become even more tightly wound in recent months. After a murder had taken place at Woolridge House—a murder Rosemary and Vera had helped solve—it seemed a fire had been lit under Evelyn. With her efforts focused solely on the impending nuptials, she was driving Vera mad.

"Now," Rosemary mused, "she's going toe-to-toe with your mother, and everyone knows Lorraine Blackburn throws the best parties. I'll bet Mother simply doesn't want to be outdone."

Uncharacteristically, Vera snapped at Rosemary. "Yes, that much has become abundantly clear. Mother's guest list has exceeded a hundred and fifty names, and she refuses to cut it to a more reasonable number. Evelyn, concerned the aisles will be lopsided, has expanded her list, and now you and Frederick have long lost cousins coming out of the woodwork."

Vera threw her hands in the air in frustration. "The last time my mother called, she couldn't decide whether we ought to choose a six-piece band or a string quartet, and I left her musing over hiring both and a great harpist besides."

Rosemary nearly chuckled, but Vera's expression of despair cured her of the inclination. "It sounds like a perfectly lovely party, aside the pop-up cousins, of course."

"You're not nearly as funny as you think you are, Rosie. The worst part is that my mother wants me to wear her dress." Vera's tone now verged on hysterical. "It's positively hideous, and she didn't even ask if I wanted it. She just assumed I'd be thrilled, and if I tell her the truth, she'll be crushed."

Vera's statement, combined with something Rosemary spotted further down the street, caused her to yank hard on Vera's arm.

"Ouch! Honestly, Rosie, I don't know what's got into you, but you're hurting me!"

"Pish posh!" Rosemary retorted in a fair imitation of Evelyn. "I've just figured out our first plan of attack. Now, come on," she said, pointing to the window of a dress shop where several fancy frocks hung on display. "We're going to find you the perfect, understated dress, and we'll force both our mothers to design the rest of the wedding fete around it!"

Stopping dead in her tracks, Vera viewed the offerings and raised one eyebrow. "None of those are really my style, Rosie," she said, backing away from the door. "They look suspiciously similar to the dress I already have no interest in wearing."

"You look as though I've just asked you to dive into a vat of boiling acid," Rosemary laughed, "rather than to participate in your favorite pastime of spending money on new clothes. Besides, I'm certain they have more styles hidden away, and if you don't find anything you like, then we'll visit every shop in London until you do. The dress always determines the type of wedding you're going to have. We can head our mothers off right here and avoid much of the fuss."

Rosemary only half-believed the assurances with which she showered her friend, knowing full well it would take nothing less than a miracle to convince either Evelyn Woolridge or Lorraine Blackburn to tone down their plans. It was worth a try even if she succeeded only in raising Vera's spirits.

Vera glared at Rosemary and crossed her arms resolutely. Undeterred, Rosemary hauled her inside, forcefully, where the slightly musty scent of linens not entirely covered by that of rose potpourri caused Vera's nose to wrinkle. Perhaps, Rosemary thought, she'd been wrong about this endeavor after all, but she made a conscious effort to breathe through her mouth and carried on as though the notion hadn't crossed her mind.

Almost immediately, a lively shopgirl descended upon the pair. "Hello, ladies. Which of you is the bride-to-be?" she asked, smiling. Her buoyant mood deflated somewhat at the sight of Vera's thinly pressed lips, and she shifted her gaze to Rosemary.

"My name is Rosemary, and this is my friend Vera," Rosemary explained, digging her elbow into Vera's ribs as a reminder to mind her manners. "Who is to be wed."

With an eye roll, Vera pasted a smile on her face. "Yes, I'm in need of a dress, but I don't as yet know precisely what style I want."

"Well, that's no trouble," the girl trilled, her sunny smile having returned. "We have a number of options, and of course, we can make alterations if you find a silhouette that appeals to you. I'll be back with some selections, and we can go from there," she said, eying Vera's slim figure with just a touch of envy.

Vera mumbled a thank you, then avoided Rosemary's gaze and wandered around the shop. She turned up her nose at a selection of Juliet Cap veils in one corner, her attention taken by a display of diamanté headpieces. "That one would look lovely on you," Rosemary said softly, pointing at a particularly lovely example, knowing her friend wouldn't be able to commit to a melancholy mood in the presence of so many sparkling baubles.

"Of course it would," Vera retorted, sticking her nose in the air for a fraction of a second before she caved, and her lips cracked into a smile.

Leaving Vera to browse, Rosemary loitered near an abandoned rack and fingered the lace of a dress bodice that reminded her of her own wedding. Thinking about that day should have been a reason to smile, but drew a frown from her instead. It had been just over a year since she'd lost her husband Andrew, suddenly, due to an undetected heart problem. Even though she'd begun to pick up the pieces of her decimated life and move on, the pain still had a way of coming back with such vengeance it sometimes caught her off guard. Tears welled in her eyes, and she brushed them away impatiently. Ruining Vera's first foray into wedding planning would not resolve the situation, and she had no intention of taking away even a piece of her dearest friend's happiness.

"All right then," the shopgirl called out, interrupting Rosemary's reverie. "I've pulled several dresses I think might suit your fancy." She appeared well relieved when she noticed Vera's demeanor had changed from irritation to moderate interest. "Why don't you try this one first?" she asked, holding out a voluminous tuft of satin and tulle with what appeared to be a nearly ten-foot-long train.

The reprieve didn't last because Vera took one look at it and her expression reverted back to a scowl. "Absolutely not," she crossed her arms resolutely and refused to budge.

When the poor girl had once again retreated into the back following Vera's veto of the rest of the selections, Rosemary— her sadness having dissolved—whirled on her friend and dished out a rare tongue lashing.

"I don't know who you are, but you need to bring back my friend. My friend who would never treat a shopgirl the way you just did. Really, Vera, you're acting positively horrendously!"

There wasn't time for Vera to retort because something across the room had caught her eye. She marched up to the till counter and picked up a framed photograph that had been resting on top. "This is it. This is the dress I want," she said, turning the picture around so Rosemary could appraise it.

"It's beautiful," Rosemary breathed after a few quiet moments. Beautiful, it was; a simple sheaf of snowy white satin covered in hand-beaded embroidered lace, with a cinched waist and a short, ruffled train. "Not exactly of the current style, but still modern and at the same time rather classic somehow. Yet, I wouldn't call it understated. This dress is a showpiece, and choosing it would give our mothers even more ammunition for throwing the ball of the century. Nevertheless, it's absolutely perfect for you!"

A genuine smile broke out across Vera's face then. "Even Mother would have to agree this gown is more appropriate than her old frock. Perhaps all hasn't been lost."

When the shopgirl reappeared, a few strands of hair stuck up on end, and her cheeks were flushed, but she'd gathered several more frocks for Vera's inspection.

"Oh, we don't need to look at any more. I've found the one I want," Vera explained, prompting the poor girl's face to twitch with the effort of holding back an irritated scowl. She held up the photograph and was met with a furrowed brow.

"I'm terribly sorry, but that's simply not possible," the girl replied.

Vera smiled. "Money is no object in this case. I'll pay handsomely, you can rest assured."

"Oh no, you misunderstand. It isn't a matter of cost," the girl replied. "You see, the dressmaker who made it has, unfortunately, passed away. That was the last dress he made, and it was for his daughter. I'm certain our new seamstress can craft something comparable. She'll be in this afternoon if you'd like to schedule a consultation."

"Hmm," Vera murmured under her breath, her eyes still trained on the picture of the dress. "I'll let you know, shall I?" Her shoulders slumped, and she left the shop looking very much like a forlorn child.

Rosemary elbowed Vera gently in the ribs. "Why not speak with the seamstress? What can it hurt?" she wanted to know.

"There's no use, Rosie. Whoever made those atrocious dresses—an insult to fashion, I tell you—isn't capable of the kind of work I'm looking for. That photograph has ruined everything." It wasn't unlike Vera to resort to dramatics. She was, after all, an actress, as Rosemary was forced to remind herself while she sighed and rolled her neck to relieve some of the tension that had settled there.

When they exited to the street to find Wadsworth standing by the car, Rosemary let out a sigh of relief. "How did you know where to find us?" she asked.

"Lucky guess, Miss," Wadsworth replied, though his usual cheerful demeanor seemed to have vanished. "Though I would have preferred not to have been forced to hunt you two ladies down. These are dangerous times we're living in, and the streets aren't safe," he pointed out, his voice full of overprotective concern.

The point well taken, Rosemary apologized. "We didn't mean to alarm you, but surely we're safe here on the high street, surrounded by throngs of other shoppers."

"That's not a risk I'm willing to take," Wadsworth replied, proving that Andrew's confidence in his abilities had been well-earned. It was he who had hired Wadsworth, accepting no other applications for the job. Rosemary found that since Andrew's passing, she'd come to appreciate his selection of butler more than she'd ever thought possible.

"Where is your haul?" Wadsworth indicated the open boot and looked around with a bewildered expression on his face.

"No bags today, Wadsworth," Vera said sullenly. "We didn't find what we were looking for."

Wadsworth's lip quirked—he'd always had a soft spot for Vera, and vice versa—but he merely closed the boot and winked at her, his irritation having ebbed. "Don't blame the shops for not being able to offer up anything comparable to your exquisiteness."

Try as she might, there wasn't a thing Vera could do to suppress the smile that spread across her face. She patted Wadsworth on the back as he held open the car door and planted a kiss on his cheek. "You're one in a million, Wads. Don't ever change."

"I don't plan on it, Miss Blackburn."

Most Definitely Murder is available now from your favorite book retailer. Keep reading for a preview of the free novella you'll get for joining my newsletter.

Enjoyed meeting Rosemary? Not ready for her story to end? If you sign up for my newsletter, you will receive The Case of the Misdelivered Valentine, a novella featuring Rosemary Lillywhite as my gift for hanging out with me.

When love is at stake, Rosemary is on the case!
In this prequel to The Case at Barton Manor, Rosemary Lillywhite solves her first case. When Rosemary receives an unexpected gift on Valentine's day, a gift that was not meant for her, she sets out to solve the mystery of the mistaken delivery.

Excerpt from The Case of the Misdelivered Valentine

Rosemary Lillywhite, draped across her settee in a deceptively languid pose, put her glass down on the end table and stubbed out the cigarette from which she had taken a single drag. The taste of tobacco coated her mouth, and she scrunched her nose in distaste. The scent was what reminded her of Andrew, anyway, and the positively acrid taste had done nothing to improve her mental state.

Rosemary had been dreading Valentine's Day ever since her maudlin mood ruined Christmas and turned New Year's Eve into a personal pity party rather than a celebration of new beginnings. Thankfully, this holiday would not inspire a spate of invitations to be regretfully declined.

Enduring such events as a widow brought on sympathetic stares from everyone who knew she'd lost her husband, not to mention platitudes offered by well-wishers who didn't understand how their condolences only made her plight all the more vivid. Instead of soothing the passing of time and the pain of growing older without the man with whom she'd expected to experience all the gifts life had to offer, their comments made barricading herself at home and avoiding all contact with the outside world a much more enticing prospect.

Valentine's Day, above all others, inspired within her a dread she could not ignore. Each year of her five with Andrew, Rosemary's front table bloomed with a big bouquet of beautiful roses—red for love, of course—tokens from her doting husband to exemplify how much she was adored. This year, there would be no roses, save for the white ones she'd draped across his headstone. White for purity, white for remembrance.

Rosemary sighed and took up the glass again to consider the inch of gin. Roses to remember, alcohol to forget. She raised the drink to her lips, then set it down with a click and another sigh as a thumping sound echoed from the front entrance through the nearby door to the parlor where she was unhappily ensconced.

"Bother," she muttered, and a moment later, she heard a familiar voice muffled by the wavy glass.

"Rosie, open up, I say." More knocking. "Where are you?"

Rather than answer, Rosemary closed her eyes and vehemently hoped her friend would just go away—a fanciful wish, as giving up simply wasn't in Vera's repertoire.

A few seconds later, the last remnants of her wish disappeared as quickly as the tendrils of smoke from the cigarette, as Vera threw open the parlor door and squinted into the darkness.

"If you wanted to keep me out, you should not have given

me a spare key." Vera said, brandishing the offending object, then tucked it carefully into her clutch. The rolling of her eyes annoyed Rosemary, who now huddled on the settee, her hair a wild mess around her face and her eyes red-rimmed from crying.

"A mistake I intend to rectify the moment my vision returns." Rosemary threw an arm up over her eyes when the drapes rattled open to let in the sun. "I suppose there's little use in asking you to leave me to my misery."

"None whatsoever." Cheerful and determined, Vera whirled around the room setting things to rights and making Rosemary tired by the simple fact of her animated presence. "You simply must stop moping, dear one," she chided.

"You're a tiresome bother to me." Yet, Rosemary was touched by the effort on her emotional behalf, and found it straining to maintain a morose manner when Vera finally plunked down upon the opposite end of the settee. "Why can't you let me have a good wallow and drown my sorrows in peace?"

Vera waved off the plea. "Where on earth is the staff? Your Wadsworth usually doesn't miss a beat, certainly not a knock at the door. The state of this room is an absolute disgrace."

"I gave them all the day off. It is a holiday, after all, and they should all be allowed to spend it with their own loved ones," Rosemary replied, her voice dull and monotone. It hadn't been easy to convince her butler or her personal maid, Anna, to leave her alone in the house, but neither the cook nor the house-keeper had protested overmuch.

"Why, it's barely noon. You mean to say this is the result of a single morning without help? What would the place look like in a week?"

The nerve of the woman, Rosemary thought, and then said in a dry tone, "Are you calling me a slob, darling? Or saying I have excellent taste in staff? I can hardly tell the difference."

There must still be a little fire left in her if she could participate in verbal volley. "Yes, well, had you insisted they stay on, you might have received news of this bouquet of roses before the blooms drowned on your front stoop." Vera reprimanded Rosemary as gently as she was able.

Rosemary pulled her arm down to really look at Vera for the first time, and saw her friend burying a pert nose in a riot of blood-red roses Her heart lurching, Rosemary felt a burst of hope as if perhaps Andrew's death and the long months alone might be nothing more than a fevered dream.

Vera set the crystal vase full of flowers down on the coffee table in front of Rosemary and handed her friend the card that had been tucked among the fragrant petals. Unable to bring herself to open the card, Rosemary merely stared at it, turning it over in her hands while fresh tears welled in her eyes. "Who on earth could have sent them?" She asked aloud.

"There's only one way to find out." Vera reached over and took the card, carefully opening it and reading aloud:

'My dearest Betty,

I still love you after all these years. My heart is filled with regret, and I wish I had been brave enough to fight for you as I should have done.

If you still feel the same way, meet me at our special place in time to watch the sunset.

I hope it's not too late, and that you'll be my Valentine today and every day forward.

Love,

JLH'

"Well," Vera breathed, "They definitely aren't for you. I wonder if they were meant for one of your neighbors."

Even in her melancholy state, Rosemary was touched by the message written on the card, and her mind raced through the names of the people who lived on her block. "There isn't a Betty on this street, I'm sure of it. Perhaps the florist made a mistake, and these flowers were supposed to go to one of the other London boroughs."

"It's possible. Why don't we call round and ask who sent them, and to what address. It would be a pity if they never reached their intended destination." Vera strode back out to the front hall where the telephone was located and beckoned for her friend to follow.

She waited for the operator to connect her to the Gold Crown Flower Shop, then explained the situation. "All right. I understand." Vera said, and hung up. "This is the intended address. The shop girl also said there was no contact information given with the order. The fellow who made the order seemed nervous, and stressed clearly that the flowers were to go to Number 8, Park Road."

"Well," Rosemary said, "The card did say *after all these years*, and we've only owned this house for the last five."

"So the gift might have been meant for some prior occupant?" Vera deduced.

Rosemary nodded, "Yes, but you must remember, this building contained a series of flats when we purchased it. We spent a simply ghastly year turning it into a townhouse. It could have been any one of those tenants. Oh—" She jumped up, the dressing gown she'd worn all day billowing around her waist.

"What is it?" Vera asked.

<hr>

The Case of the Misdelivered Valentine is only available by signing up for my newsletter. Keep reading for an explanation of the British English terms and slang used in the book!